Journey through the Night

Anne DeVries

Journey through the Night

2. The darkness deepens

PAIDEIA PRESS
St. Catharines, Ontario, Canada

First published in Dutch as *Reis door de Nacht*, © G.F.
Callenbach B.V. of Nijkerk. Translated by Harry der
Nederlanden. Illustrations by Anthony Hedrick.

ISBN 0-88815-752-5
Printed in the United States of America.

THE DARKNESS DEEPENS

CHAPTER ONE

Maybe it was because of the stormy weather, but on this March morning in 1942 Fritz was overflowing with vitality as wild and uncontrollable as the wind. Yesterday's storm still had a hold on Fritz's companions too, it seemed, as he led them speeding on their bikes into town, yelling and screaming and performing crazy stunts. At the school yard their elation resulted in a big free-for-all. Then suddenly everyone was silent. Crossing the school yard was Mr. Wiesel, a short, stocky man with a goatee. He taught history and German at the school, and the students called him "The Boer." This was his first day back at school after a two-week illness. No one was certain what had been wrong with him. Some said he'd had bronchitis, but others said it was a nervous breakdown. Most students believed the latter.

When Fritz spotted the teacher approaching the school an idea popped into his head. Immediately he blurted it out to the other boys: "Let's give the old 'Boer' such a hard time in class today that he stays home for another two weeks!"

His friends weren't as enthusiastic about the plan as he was, Fritz noticed. But nobody objected so he ignored their hesitation. No one liked Mr. Wiesel for he was said to be a Nazi sympathizer and a traitor and it was becoming clearer day by day that all the other teachers in the school were "sound."

At the beginning of every class, Mr. Willems, the school headmaster, would tap out the letter "V" in Morse code—three short and one long tap. This was how every broadcast from England began with the Morse code "V" which stood for victory.

Mr. Vander Brook, the literature teacher, never missed a chance to make a joke at the expense of the Germans. He even had the daring to openly discuss war news in class but, of course, he personally knew all the families of his students and was sure they were "sound." Once he'd come to class with a list of supposedly foreign names for the Fuehrer, Adolph Hitler. His Russian title for Hitler was Nokisblokoff, his Chinese title, Hisa Lu Sah, and so on. Several times, also, he had brought anti-German poems and other patriotic literature to school. The other teachers, however, were more careful.

For example, Fritz's art teacher Mr. Biemolt, was extremely cautious. Even in his morning prayers he no longer dared mention the government-in-exile. Nevertheless, he was a loyal, trustworthy man. Once, when Fritz had been agonizing for sometime over a difficult drawing, the teacher had come up beside his desk and asked him: "Well, how's it going, Fritz?"

Fritz had looked up brightly and said: "Great, sir! Tonight there'll be another squadron of English planes over the German Ruhr."

Mr. Biemolt had burst out laughing, but then had cast an apprehensive glance at the open door, for Mr. Wiesel was teaching just across the hall.

No one trusted Mr. Wiesel. He wasn't really a bad man though, and before the war, everyone had liked him. But ever since the Germans had invaded the country, everyone shunned him because his love for Germany and his hostility toward England were common knowledge. As a result his name had become a dirty word. He was not a member of the Dutch Nazi Movement, but people said he'd gone door to door collecting for Winter Help, the German relief agency. As if they couldn't take care of their own!

Several months ago the Germans had ordered everyone in town to turn in all their copper articles. Most people had quickly buried everything they had that was made of copper, because they knew it would be used to make German ammunition. Mr. Wiesel, however, had dutifully turned in all his copper to the Germans. Sometimes, too, he had been seen in town with a German officer, who had even visited his home occasionally. Who knows what information-he was passing on to the German, the townfolk asked each other. Perhaps he was secretly spying for the Nazis. It was hard for Fritz to feel sorry for the man, even if he had been very ill. It was difficult to put up with him at school as a teacher, but the school board could do nothing, for no matter how much they wanted to, they couldn't fire him for his pro-German tendencies. The other teachers could make him an outcast, but that was about all. The students, on the other hand, could make life impossible for him in the classroom, suggested Fritz, and then he might stay home voluntarily.

"It will be like being part of the resistance movement," he encouraged the others. "What do you say, guys? We'll drive him crazy! I'll start, but you have to help. I know what! Has anybody got a pin or button with the Queen or the flag on it? Here, let me have it. This will get his goatee, just wait and see!"

Several boys were able to dig patriotic symbols out of their pockets: a pin made from a quarter, which carried the Queen's silhouette; a bracelet made from pennies, which were also impressed with the Queen's likeness; a couple of necklaces made with red, white, and blue beads; and an orange bandana which symbolized the House of Orange. Fritz put everything in his pockets. Then the sound of the school bell shrilled across the school yard, fluttering and stuttering on the wind. The children headed for their classes. Among them was the young and innocent face of Fritz De Boer.

The first two classes progressed uneventfully. Mr. Vander Brook told a couple of anti-German jokes that he learned from a Dutch worker. The man, who had been sent to work in a German munition factory, had been given a few days of leave to see his family.

Six months ago, the German-run Labor Office had ordered this man to report to the German factory.

Unemployed, he could not refuse the order to work, else all public support for him would have been cut off and his family left to starve. With this threat over their heads more than a hundred thousand workers had been forced to go to work in German factories. Although they went reluctantly and worked as slowly as possible, they nevertheless helped the German war effort.

But, as Mr. Vander Brook pointed out, there were also many who refused to go. He didn't explain, but Fritz knew what he meant. Increasing numbers of workers were defying the German authorities, many because they realized it was becoming dangerous to be in Germany as a result of the nightly bombing raids made by English planes. Often, the drafted workers tried to get an exemption, but if that didn't work, they would go into hiding with friends in some other part of the country.

Their families were cared for with money and ration cards received from the underground, the organized resistance movement. This was not something people gossiped about, for it could be dangerous. Everyone knew, though, that the underground existed and that it went about its work quietly and efficiently.

The workers on leave had told Mr. Vander Brook that there was also a resistance movement in Germany. Many Germans hated Hitler also.

"Who knows what's in store for him!" said Mr. Vander Brook. "But that's enough for now. Let's get back to work."

Fritz had trouble keeping his mind on his grammar exercises. Who knows? Last year, too, there had been rumors of a brewing revolt in Germany. Maybe if the English and Americans came now, it would cause a revolution there. As soon as the Allied invasion started, that would be the end of the Third Reich, Fritz reasoned. Then would follow the Day of the Axe, when the heads of all Nazi traitors and collaborators would roll. "Wiesel's too," he thought with anticipation. "Today we'll give him a sample of what's to come. But will the others back me up? I'd better remind them again after class," he told himself.

But Fritz didn't get that chance. As Mr. Vander Brook gathered his papers and books to leave the room, Mr. Wiesel walked in. They passed each other at the door.

"Good morning, Vander Brook," said Mr. Wiesel. But Mr. Vander Brook didn't reply. He didn't even look at Mr. Wiesel. Taking an exaggerated step aside, he let the other teacher enter the room. Then he left without having said a word.

Immediately the class became very still. Mr. Wiesel flushed angrily. With lips compressed, he walked to the desk. Putting his briefcase on it, he turned to the class and said, "Good morning, class."

A mumble came from the class.

"Huzzah!" cried Fritz. It was the greeting used by the Dutch Nazi Movement. He saw Mr. Wiesel glance up, startled. But that was all. Mr. Wiesel took his books from his briefcase and began the lesson. They were studying the conflicts preceding the Synod of Dordt. Fritz pretended to be listening attentively, but meanwhile he was digging in his pockets for the forbidden jewelry. He slipped the bracelet on his wrist, and the pin with the Queen's head on his lapel.

When Mr. Wiesel turned to the board to write down some dates, Fritz hung the red, white, and blue necklace around his neck and tucked the orange bandana into his shirt pocket. When he was all decked out, he sat up straight to flaunt his colorful decorations. Mr. Wiesel didn't even blink an eye when he turned around. Was he near-sighted? Or was he just pretending not to see? Maybe he was too involved in what he was teaching. He was a spell-binding history teacher Fritz had to admit. At the moment he was telling about the political importance of the union of the Arminian and Calvinist factions during the seventeenth century. "But there are always a few mavericks determined to go their own way," Mr. Wiesel explained.

Fritz heaved a loud sigh. Mr. Wiesel didn't seem to hear him. Fritz took the orange bandana out of his pocket and fanned himself with it. Then he tucked it back into his pocket. "There! That should do it!" he thought.

"Is something bothering you, Fritz?" Mr. Wiesel asked in an exasperated tone.

"Who, me?" Fritz asked innocently. "Why, no! What makes you think something's bothering me? Sir?"

He had expected to hear laughter from his buddies, but there was only suspenseful silence. He decided to lay it on a little thicker.

"I'm just as sound as can be, sir. I wish everyone was as sound as me." Fritz stressed the word "sound." People had begun distinguishing between those who were "sound" and those who were "soft"—the people who were loyal to the government-in-exile, as opposed to those "soft" towards Nazism.

Fritz heard a ripple of laughter in the classroom. But Mr. Wiesel quashed it with a glance.

"Then sit still," Mr. Wiesel said unruffled. "And take off all that junk! You look like a sideshow freak."

The whole class was grinning at Fritz now. "Those jerks! Whose side were they on anyway?" Fritz was starting to boil.

"Junk?" he said. "Junk? Maybe it's junk to you, but to me these are the prettiest colors in the world. Right guys?"

Turning to the class, he brandished his bandana. A couple of his friends straightened up and nodded. But that was all. Then the clear voice of Gracie Bemmelman piped up, "Attaboy Fritz! Three cheers for the Queen!"

"Oso!" cried Fritz. "Orange Shall Overcome!"

"Fine!" said Mr. Wiesel. "You've had your demonstration. Now, if you please, take off those trinkets. Otherwise you'll be picked up when you go outside."

"Better watch out you don't get picked up yourself," Fritz shot back insolently.

That hit home. Fritz saw Mr. Wiesel's eyes flash behind his glasses. He came and stood right in front of Fritz. In an ominously calm voice, he demanded: "What do you mean by that? Come on, out with it!"

Fritz would have preferred to stop, but the whole class was looking on. He took a deep breath, and in the strained silence, pressed on: "You know what I mean. Pretty soon the Allies will be here and then comes the

Day of the Axe."

The class was absolutely still for several seconds. Fritz could sense their reaction. He had gone too far!

It was too late now to take back what he'd said. He looked up into the strained, pale face of his teacher. At the same time a strong hand seized him by the collar and his beads clattered to the floor. Fritz felt himself being lifted from his seat and propelled toward the door. His feet barely touched the floor. Little Wiesel was as strong as an ox! Fritz went sailing out into the hall.

"And stay there until after class!" he heard the controlled voice say behind him. "Then we'll talk again."

The door slammed shut. Fritz's ears were ringing, or was it the wind blowing in the trees? He couldn't tell. The left side of his face stung. Had Wiesel given him a clout on the head? Strange! It all seemed so unreal. It had happened though. He'd been put out in the hall like a naughty little boy. He'd lost the battle with the teacher. His whole plan had fizzled. "It wasn't my fault," he raged to himself. "It's because of those cowards in there who didn't back me up." Fritz could have bawled in anger and wounded pride. Furiously he kicked the classroom door, but he heard only the drone of Mr. Wiesel's teaching voice. More than likely he hadn't even noticed. Further down the hall though a door did open. Mr. Willems, the school principal, was on his way to the office. Fritz ducked. A good thing Mr. Willems hadn't seen him, Fritz thought, otherwise he'd have had some explaining to do. Willems wouldn't back him up either. "They're all cowards! That's why the Krauts and their cronies have everything their way," Fritz told himself.

With trembling fingers he ripped off the bracelet and his other trinkets, and in a fit of temper flung them down the hall.

When the class was over, his buddies approached him and asked for the things they had lent him. Fritz just glared at them. Mr. Wiesel came out into the hall to fetch him, but he could sense that as yet there could be no reasoning with Fritz. He simply told Fritz to stay in during recess and work on his history lesson. But Fritz thought, "I'll be darned if I write a single word!" He sat on the window sill and stared outside. In the school yard he could see Mr. Wiesel strolling along with Mr. Biemolt, another one of those cowards! Fritz strode across the room to the blackboard and angrily picked up a piece of chalk. He hesitated a moment. Should he? Why not? What did he care what they did to him! He didn't give up so easily.

Written on the board was a column of dates, the last two read:

> 1609—Death of Arminius
> 1619—Synod of Dordt

Fritz added one more:

> 1942—Liberation and death of Adolph Hitler and Wiebe Wiesel.

"A stroke of genius!" thought Fritz, and sat down to await the results. Again and again he had to suppress the fear which kept welling up in his chest. He was no coward! He searched through his pockets for the cigarette butt he'd picked up somewhere. To top off his defiance, he put the butt in his mouth and lit it. Students were not allowed to smoke on the school grounds, much less in the school itself.

From his back pocket he pulled out a leaflet that he had been given the day before by a farm worker. It was called "The Whirlwind" and was supposed to have been dropped from an English plane. On the front page there was a picture of Churchill with a pugnacious look on his face and his fingers held up in a V for victory. Printed beside the picture was a speech Churchill had delivered to the English parliament. It would cost much blood and tears to defeat the Nazis, Churchill had stressed, but the Allies would fight on to the very end even if it were to take years, Fritz read. "That Churchill was always such a pessimist!" he thought.

An article on the next page told about a secret peace overture made by the Germans, which the Allies had summarily rejected. Another article described the bombing in the Ruhr Valley of Germany where most of its weapon factories were located. Large numbers of German submarines had also been destroyed, the article said. And the United States, which had entered the war on December 7, was building a huge invasion force.

"Sure as shooting, they'll come sometime this year," Fritz told himself, "and then they'll make short work of the Germans! Churchill will be pleasantly surprised. Unless the old fox only said such things to stir up the English people."

The bell rang. Fritz quickly put the paper back into his pocket and doused his cigarette in a flower pot. He crossed his arms and sat back in his chair as the class filed into the room. There was Mr. Wiesel. No one dared to say anything. Mr. Wiesel looked at Fritz. Was there a glimmer of hope in his eyes? He said nothing about Fritz's uncompleted assignment.

"Quiet, please," asked Mr. Wiesel. "The bell has rung! Let's open our books."

"Ask not for whom the bell tolls; it tolls for thee," Fritz quoted under his breath. But no one laughed. The room was filled with whispers and all eyes were riveted on the blackboard. Mr. Wiesel turned too, to see what all the fuss was about. He snatched an eraser and obliterated the last line with an angry swipe.

Then he stood silently with his back turned to the class for what seemed like a very long time. When again he faced the class he spoke in a quivering voice to Fritz: "You're expelled for the rest of the week. You tell your father I'll see him tomorrow evening."

"Whatever you say," answered Fritz in an insolent voice. With calculated slowness, he packed his books into his knapsack.

Mr. Wiesel stood waiting with apparent calm. But suddenly he snapped: "I'd advise you to hurry, before I do something we'll both regret!"

Fritz looked up. The expression on Mr. Wiesel's face frightened him, and he was greatly relieved when he reached the safety of the hall. Quietly he tiptoed to the front door, hoping to avoid a questioning by the principal. Outside, he swung the knapsack over his shoulder, unlocked his bike, and began pedaling for home. A feeling of foreboding made his legs seem very heavy.

At the intersection leading out of town, two policemen were checking identifications. For the past

year everyone over fifteen had to carry with him a card
with his photograph, name, address, and fingerprints.
Fritz hoped they would stop him too, but the men must
have been able to see he was only fourteen for they let
him pass. This didn't do anything to help Fritz's morale
either.

"Boy, it was cold!" Fritz thought as he pedaled
along. It was almost April, but winter was slow leaving
this year. Hitler must now be regretting his declaration
of war on Russia last summer. At first the fighting had
gone in Hitler's favor, Fritz recalled. The German army
had penetrated deep into Russia. But now German
soldiers were freezing by the thousands on the wind-
swept Russian steppes. More and more German soldiers
were being sent to the Russian front, so that the west
coast was left almost undefended.

"The English and Americans should have an easy
time of it," thought Fritz. He wished they would attack
Germany right now, with everything they had. "They'd
better come soon," Father had said, "because the Germans are carrying everything out of the country: cattle,
food, equipment, and more and more of our people."

Now he was riding on the unsheltered country road
past the outskirts of the town, and the wind hit him head
on. He had to stand up and put his full weight on the
pedals to get anywhere.

An open army truck loaded with German soldiers
passed him. The men sat in two rows facing each other,
their collars up over their ears and their rifles between their
knees. "What's the matter guys;" Fritz thought to himself.
"You think it's cold here? Just wait 'til you get to Russia!"

Lately, the German troops seemed to be constantly shifting from place to place. The high school was being used to bivouac German soldiers for the second time since the start of the war. John and Tricia, his older brother and sister, had been home all week as a result. Well, now he could stay home all week too. But what would Father say when he told him what had happened? The question nagged at Fritz and made him more anxious the closer he got to home. The nearer he got, the more certain he became that he was in for a scorching from Father. He took a breather behind a barn along the road. There he tried to rehearse the story he would tell Father. But suddenly he became disgusted with himself. He resolved to tell the whole truth. Whatever else he was, he was not a liar! He was far from perfect—wild and harebrained—but he had never tried to deceive his parents. Having made up his mind, he jumped on his bike and raced home as fast as he could to get the matter over and done with.

CHAPTER TWO

When Fritz was only a few hundred yards from home, something so startled him that he stopped pedaling. And because the wind was so strong, it halted him in his tracks and he toppled over, bike and all. A monstrous apparition, a huge grey balloon, came speeding past the house only a few feet above the ground. It sailed across the road and suddenly straightened up, as a cable dragging along behind snagged in the power lines alongside the road.

Blue sparks crackled along the cable until the huge balloon jerked itself loose and sped away once more. A little farther on, it again snagged, this time in the branches of a large oak in the neighbor's pasture.

Father and John came running across the lawn, with old Uncle Gerrit not far behind. People also came running out of the neighbor's house. But Fritz had a head start on everybody. Nemo, his dog, passed him and got to the oak tree first. He grabbed the wildly flapping cable between his teeth and hung on, growling. Fritz grabbed it too and looked around for a post or tree on which to anchor it.

"Hold on! Hold on, Fritz!" yelled John as he raced up to help.

But Fritz didn't have to be told. He wasn't about to let go! Not even when a sudden gust freed the balloon from the tree and carried it away once more. Fritz was dragged along, but he held on in the hope that his brother would catch up any moment. But John had pulled up, startled when the balloon had broken free, and now it was going much too fast for him to catch up. Even Nemo was having trouble keeping up.

Fritz gritted his teeth and fought to regain his feet. He succeeded for a moment, taking huge loping steps across the pasture, across a sizeable canal, and into another field. But suddenly he was spun around like a top and a violent gust of wind lifted him into the air. When Fritz saw the ground dropping away beneath his feet, he decided he had had enough, and he let go of the cable.

He fell into a freshly-plowed field from a height of several yards and did a couple of somersaults before he came to rest on his knees, staring after the balloon. It went speeding across the fields, past a horse that went stampeding off in fright, past another farmhouse where it was pursued by more people, and then across more pastureland toward the horizon.

Meanwhile, John had caught up with his brother and, still panting, began brushing him off. Father also arrived, asking Fritz anxiously if he had been hurt.

When they were assured he was all right, they had a good laugh because Fritz had made such a ludicrous picture, leap-frogging along at the end of the cable. Then, with Nemo still barking with excitement, they strolled back to Uncle Gerrit, who had been stopped by one of the narrow, water-filled ditches separating the fields.

"Hey, Fritz," he shouted. "How come you didn't bring back that little balloon for me? I wanted to play with it too." Their neighbor, Harry Hoeks, joined them in the field, and the small group stood with their backs to the wind, talking.

"It was an English barrage balloon," said Father, "that must have broken loose in the storm yesterday." London was surrounded by such balloons, he explained. They forced enemy planes to approach the city at an elevation where they could be spotted and shot down more easily. Once before, a southwest wind had sent one of these balloons scudding over the neighborhood.

"If you'd held on a little longer," said Hoeks, elbowing Fritz, "you'd be in Germany by now!"

"Yeah. And it's easy enough to end up in Germany, even without co-operating," added Uncle Gerrit. But then he slapped Fritz on the back. "Still, you're a real fighter, my boy. Once you latch onto something, you don't let go very quick!"

Then they were forced to head for home, because the wind blew their words back into their mouths. Fritz had to pick up his bike first, so he was the last one to get to the house. His sister Tricia met him on the path in front of the house, her long hair flying in the wind. She refused to move out of his way, and they jostled and shoved each other for possession of the path.

Mother watched them from the window, laughing, with little Hans in her arms. Little Hans, the baby of the family, was almost eighteen months old now. He was a cute little toddler. When Fritz stopped in front of the window, Hansie held out his arms and then kicked and squealed with delight as Fritz made funny faces at the window. Fritz was crazy about his baby brother, as were the others. He coaxed Hansie to give him a kiss through the window and laughed uproariously as the little snub nose flattened against the glass. Then he wheeled his bike to the garage.

Inside the garage, Father, John, and Uncle Gerrit were busy making parcels of rye bread, bacon, and dried beans for relatives and friends living in the large cities. Uncle Gerrit was doing the weighing, John the wrapping, and Father was addressing the parcels. The Germans had just reduced everyone's rations again. In the cities, many people were beginning to suffer from hunger. But because the De Boers lived out in the country among the farmers, they could still get plenty of everything.

"Did you get out early today, Fritz?" asked John. And when Fritz nodded, he said, "Great! Then you can come along this afternoon. Father's going somewhere with the car, and Tricia's coming along too. Right, Dad?"

"Keen!" said Fritz. "But . . . well . . . Dad, I got kicked out of school today. And I'm not supposed to come back until next week."

There! He'd done it! Father's hands stopped what they were doing. Fritz didn't dare look up, but he knew what he would see in Father's eyes: disappointment, sadness, worry. If he had only thought of this moment before he had forced the showdown with Wiesel.

"Who kicked you out?"

"Mr. Wiesel, Dad."

"Let's go to the studio," Father said to him. Turning to the others, he said, "You can finish without me. Don't forget to add that address to the list. You know which one."

"Good luck—to both of you," said Uncle Gerrit with a grin. He saw the humorous side to everything, no matter how serious.

Fritz followed Father to the studio. The blueprints that had been on the drawing board several weeks ago were still there. Father didn't do much work these days. There were very few homes being built now.

"Okay, let's hear your story," said Father as they sat down opposite each other. "Start at the beginning and don't leave anything out."

So Fritz gave a blow-by-blow description of the whole affair. Now that he was forced to review the incident under Father's serious gaze, it appeared in a wholly different light. He had let himself get carried away. He had gone too far! But he still thought that he had the right idea: "Wiesel shouldn't be allowed to teach in our school anymore. If he likes the Germans so well, he should go to Germany and work in the factories," Fritz told Father.

"So! You think he doesn't belong in your school any

more?" said Father. "What has he done in school that makes him unfit to be your teacher? Has he defended the Nazis in class? Has he spoken out against the Queen and the government?"

"No, not in class," admitted Fritz. "But everybody knows where he stands."

"That's none of your business," said Father. "He has the right to think as he pleases. In a free country he also has the right to say what he thinks. And if you deny him that right, you're no better than the Nazis. They don't allow anyone free speech either. Besides, the man is your teacher, so you owe him respect, and you should obey him when you're in his class.

"If he says something you don't agree with, then you have the right to disagree, politely and with humility. After all, you're still an ignorant little boy. What you did today was stupid and vicious and childish! You numbskull! Your buddies left you holding the bag. You played the clown and the daredevil for them. If the weather weren't so bad, I'd send you back right now to straighten things out with Mr. Wiesel."

"But, Dad," sputtered Fritz, "he's a traitor! Everybody says . . . ."

"I know! And most of what 'everybody says' is gossip and rubbish!" Father exploded. "You can't believe everything you hear, Fritz. Not by a long shot! I've known Mr. Wiesel for a long time. He's an honest, reliable man with a strong sense of justice. I don't believe he'd ever side with the Nazis. And if you condemn him without proof, you're acting just like the Nazis. In some places they've even lined up people against the wall and shot them without any proof of guilt. The Nazis don't have any sympathy for convictions other than their own. But I expect otherwise from you! You know what I think? I think that Mr. Wiesel may just have a hatred for the English."

"Oh, sure. I know that," said Fritz. "He doesn't try to hide it."

"Right! And he has his reasons. I guess I've never told you anything about him, have I? He was born in South Africa. His father was from the Transvaal."

"Oh, that's why they sometimes call him 'The Boer'!" remarked Fritz.

"They still call him that? We called him that too, when I went to high school here. It was an honorable nickname in those days. His father was killed by the English during the Boer Wars, and he and his mother were prisoners in an English concentration camp.

"You've probably heard the story of how the English imprisoned thousands of women and children in order to make the Boers stop fighting. Quite a few died of starvation and sickness. After the war, his mother came to the Netherlands to join her family. But she never recovered from those days in that English concentration camp. She died young."

Fritz listened attentively, impressed by Father's story.

"Did the English really do that?" he asked.

Father nodded.

"Now do you understand why he hates the English? It may not be right, but it's understandable. We shouldn't hate anybody, not even a nationality. You may hate evil and injustice, in fact you should. But not the English or the Germans. And Mr. Wiesel should know by now that the Germans are guilty of the same things he hates the English for.

"The Germans also have their concentration camps, and they certainly don't treat their prisoners any better than the English did. War sometimes makes people more vicious than animals. We've got to be careful that doesn't happen to us, Fritz. I'll tell you what. We'll go and see Mr. Wiesel tonight and save him the long trip out here. First, you'll apologize for your behavior and then I'll talk to him. Okay?"

Fritz nodded.

"Fritz, my boy," said Father with a sigh. "You've got to learn to think things through. You've got to think of the consequences. Fritz, if you don't change your ways, you're going to cause yourself all kinds of grief."

"I'll try, Dad. I'm sorry," said Fritz. And he meant it. Poor Mr. Wiesel! He had insulted the man terribly. In his imagination, Fritz saw Mr. Wiesel as a pale, thin boy, standing with a frail woman behind a barbed-wire fence. "What if all that had happened to me?" Fritz asked himself.

Suddenly Father leaped to his feet. "Look at the time! Come on, we're going to miss it!"

Fritz immediately understood what Father was referring to. He dashed into the living room and turned on the radio. Meanwhile, Father had called Uncle Gerrit and John and they came hurrying into the room. Mr. Hoeks also came tagging along. He didn't own a radio himself, so he dropped in every day to listen to the news at the De Boers.

They were just in time; the beep, beep, beep, bee-eep that introduced the broadcast was just ending. While Mother put little Hans to bed, and Tricia and Margy set the table, everyone else gathered around to listen to Radio Orange, the voice of the Dutch government-in-exile from London.

Despite its being strictly forbidden, in homes all across the German-occupied territories people were assembled around their radios to listen to the broadcasts from England. In the De Boer country home there was little risk, for there was little chance any authorities would catch them in the act. Although the Germans tried to interfere with the broadcasts by jamming the frequency, the messages were still intelligible.

This time there was nothing special on the news. On the Russian front, said the announcer, the Germans had been forced to retreat by Russian ski troops. A large American steamship that the Germans claimed to have sunk had arrived safely in England with a huge cargo of supplies. Then there was some sketchy news about Indonesia. The Dutch colony had shared the fate of Holland. It too had been conquered, but by a different enemy. It had fallen into Japanese hands three months before.

The day after Japan had made its treacherous attack on Pearl Harbor, the Netherlands had declared war on Japan. The Dutch navy managed to sink quite a few Japanese ships before it was virtually wiped out in the battle of the Java Sea at the end of February. Fritz still remembered the shock and despair on everyone's faces when the terrible news became known. Now the announcer was saying that the stubborn resistance of the Dutch forces in Indonesia had increased Australia's chances for survival.

As they ate, they discussed the latest news. But mother paid little attention to the table talk; she kept looking outside. Big snowflakes were beginning to whip by the window.

"Are you sure you have to go out on a day like this?" she asked Father anxiously.

"Yes," said Father, "I've got appointments I can't break. Two families in Zwolle are counting on having roast turkey this coming Sunday, and I can't very well disappoint them. I mean, for these people a Sunday without a turkey just wouldn't be a Sunday."

Fritz looked up at Father. Father spoke in a very serious tone, but he certainly couldn't *be* serious! Uncle Gerrit couldn't resist adding that it was perfect weather for delivering turkeys: "It won't be so stifling hot in the trunk, so our turkeys can travel in comfort." Then Fritz knew that the trip had some other purpose — one that was not to be discussed. Fritz had learned not to ask questions when there were mysterious goings-on around the house.

He kept his eyes peeled, however, when John drove the car out of the garage after dinner. But then Uncle Gerrit called him to lend a hand in catching a couple of turkeys. The wary birds seemed to sense their intent, however, and scattered frantically every time the old man approached. The cocks eyed him suspiciously, gobbling their indignation. Uncle Gerrit had raised chickens before, but never turkeys, and he loathed the ornery birds. He had named them all after prominent Nazis.

"Who'll we take this time?" said the old man, with a gleam in his eye. "Don't get so huffy, Herr Hitler! You may be able to intimidate your comrades that way, but it doesn't impress me in the slightest. I can see right through you! The louder you gobble, the more of a chicken you are. But your time hasn't come yet.

"I think big fat Goering over there is about ready. Here, Herman, come and reap your reward. You boasted there would never be an English plane over Germany, and now they're flattening the whole country. Hold on to him, Fritz! He's a slippery customer! Who should we pick to keep him company? How about Goebbels there? He's full of gobbledygook. And, now, how about a lady to round out the party? There's Eva Braun. Come here, Eva, honey . . . ."

So Uncle Gerrit and Fritz stuffed the Minister of the Air Force and the Minister of Propaganda into the trunk of the DKW along with Hitler's mistress. There they sat, grumbling in the dark, as the car pulled out of the driveway under Mother's worried eyes. Tricia had decided to stay home to keep her company. And with the weather turning so cold and nasty, Hanneke might need someone to walk her home from school this afternoon.

Fritz, however, was going along with Father. He sat perched on the edge of the back seat in anticipation. He didn't deserve to go, Mother had said, after she'd heard about his exploits at school. And Fritz knew she was right. He threw a grateful look at his father. His strong hands rested confidently on the steering wheel. Fritz was glad he had this man for his father. He might be strict, but he didn't hold anything against you for very long. Now that their talk was behind them and Fritz had promised to do better, everything was forgiven.

CHAPTER THREE

The wipers could hardly keep pace with the wet snow being plastered against the windshield. Sometimes, when the wind came blasting around a farm building or a clump of trees, the car would suddenly lurch sideways across the road. But Father seemed to be in an exceptionally good mood, for he sat behind the wheel whistling "She'll be comin' round the mountain." Suddenly, however, he was fighting the wheel as the car bucked first one way and then the other. Quickly, he pulled over to the shoulder.

"Those lousy tires!" he said. "I bet we've got another flat. Let's take a quick look-see."

It was the right front wheel. Fritz grabbed the jack, and John was already getting out the spare. A few minutes later they had changed the tire and were on their way again. But before another half hour had passed, they were pulling over again with a flat rear tire. This time, however, they were in the middle of a large village, only a few hundred meters from a garage. Together they pushed the car to the garage, and Father honked the horn. But no one showed up, so they opened the garage door themselves and shouldered the car inside.

A disgruntled-looking fellow in dirty blue overalls sauntered toward them, saying nothing. He eyed the DKW contemptuously and then fixed the same look on them. When Father asked him if he had time to fix a couple of tires, he grumbled: "Do I have a choice? We're really too busy with other things for such small jobs. Before we get our cars running, we have a lot more to worry about than flat tires!"

"I thought this was a garage," said Father.

"More like a blacksmith shop and a gas factory," the man replied, pointing to an old Chevrolet on which he was putting a gas generator. "A garage repairs cars, but around here they've all been impounded by the Germans," he continued bitterly. "On the other hand, there are always a few people who still ride in style and have access to gasoline—like those big shots who're here to impound our horses. You with them?"

"No, we're not," said Father. "You've got us all wrong. Whatever you're thinking, you're wrong. Understand? Oso!"

The mechanic studied Father for a moment.

"We'll see," he said. "Leave it here and come back in about an hour."

"He thought we were collaborators," said John when they got outside.

"I don't blame him," replied Father.

It did seem strange that, while almost all cars had been impounded by the Germans, Father had managed to keep the DKW and had even obtained a generous gasoline allowance for it. John and Fritz had also looked on in surprise when, after standing on blocks for almost two years, the DKW had come rolling out of the garage, ready to go. Father had obtained an automobile permit from the occupying government.

John could guess what had happened: the official who had to approve automobile permits was "sound" and had issued a permit to Father so he could use the little DKW for resistance work. Nevertheless, John was bothered by the suspicious looks people sent their way whenever they drove by. He could see scorn in their eyes. And once, when the car had been left parked along the curb for half an hour, some youngster had traced a swastika in the dust on the door.

Now they were stranded in a strange village for at least an hour, and the already bad weather was getting worse. First they strolled to a nearby church to admire the architecture. Father was interested in old churches and this one was several hundred years old. But wind always seems to blow strongest around churches and it cut through their coats, chilling them to the bone. They walked on at a brisk pace, trying to keep warm, until they came to the town square, which was filled with farmers and horses.

"This must be where they're impounding the horses," said Father. Inspectors accompanied by German officers moved from horse to horse as their owners stood by holding their animals for inspection.

"Come on," said Father. "Let's steer clear of this. We'll see if we can find a cafe and get a cup of something hot."

Not far down the street was a large restaurant, but as they were about to enter, Father suddenly did an about-face. "Come on," he said, pushing them back. "We're not going in there!"

"Why? What's the matter?" asked Fritz.

"Didn't you see the sign on the door?" said John.

Taped on the inside of the door were the words, WE DON'T SERVE JEWS.

"So?" said Fritz. "We're not Jews!"

Fritz could be a bit thick-headed at times, and often he opened his mouth before thinking.

"You mean you'd give your business to a man who persecutes Jews?" asked John.

Then Fritz caught on. "Of course not! A creep like that isn't going to make a penny off me!"

"I wish everyone felt that way," said Father, "but most people don't seem to pay any attention. Even the movie theaters are filled every night, though they all have those signs stuck on the doors. One night at a concert in Amersfoort, at the beginning, it was announced that all Jews would have to leave, and guess what happened? Everybody got up and walked out, except for a few German soldiers and Dutch Nazis. What do you think of that?"

"Neat!" exclaimed Fritz. "Where did you hear that?"

"It's better you don't know. And be careful! If you tell the story to someone else, don't tell them where you heard it. But I know it's true."

"There's another cafe," said John, pointing across the street.

"Another German boot-licker!" added Fritz, seeing the sign on the door.

"You'd think there would be one cafe owner in this town who isn't hand in glove with the Germans," grumbled Father.

"Maybe they can't get any supplies unless they put up those signs," suggested John.

"Then they ought to shut down," said Father emphatically. "If we all stood up for the Jews, then maybe the Nazis wouldn't dare persecute them. I'm afraid there's a lot of hardship ahead for these people if the war doesn't end soon. These signs are only a nuisance compared with what's happening elsewhere, and it's coming here too, I'm afraid."

"I'll bet the invasion will be this spring," proclaimed Fritz.

"I surely hope so!" Father said fervently.

They turned down the street that led back to the garage. There they saw an old farmhouse that had been converted into a restaurant. They approached it hopefully. But again it was posted.

The two boys stepped off the porch, but Father stayed by the door. He was peering through the window, whistling to himself. He eyed the sign and whistled a few more bars.

"Come on!" he said, motioning to John and Fritz, and stepped inside. Fritz followed at his heels, but John hesitated until he saw that the sign had suddenly vanished. Father turned around and motioned again, grinning. "Come on! It's okay! Everybody's welcome here, and it's nice and warm inside."

They sat down close to the old stove, chuckling because the offending sign had been tucked away inside Father's overcoat.

"Shhh!" said Father as the proprietor approached. "Shape up!"

The man asked what they wanted. "How about some coffee," he suggested, when they didn't order right away.

"Coffee?" said Father. "You mean that ersatz stuff? No thanks! We're too young for that brew. We're only a bunch of kids! Just give us each a glass of hot milk."

As the proprietor was bringing them their hot milk, three farmers entered the room and hurried over to the stove. One of them, an old man, sat down close to Father and sighed deeply.

"Cold, isn't it?" said Father.

The man nodded vigorously.

"Things not going so good?"

"It's madness, that's what it is! What's a man to do?"

"They take away your horse?"

"My best one. A three-year-old gelding."

"Didn't they give you a good price?"

"What good does that do me when it comes time to plow? We're going to be late this year as it is, and now I've got only one horse left—a nag that's about ready for the glue factory. And then they ask you to produce more! Tell me, how am I going to do that without a decent horse? Farmers always get the short end of the stick!"

"Oh, I don't know," said Father soothingly. "At least you've got plenty to eat. In the cities, people are starving."

But the man wasn't listening. He was too wrapped up in his own woes. Pensively, he lit his pipe. But what on earth was he smoking? A sharp stench filled the cafe. It smelled like horse manure!

"And when you read the paper," he began again, "they make all kinds of promises. Yesterday, for example. . . ."

"What paper do you read?" asked Father.

"*Race and Nation,*" said the farmer. "And the *Farm Journal,* of course."

"How come you read that National Socialist paper? You a member of the National Socialist Movement?"

"Sure, why not?" answered the man. "Everybody around here was joining, so why shouldn't I? They had a good program for the farmers. At least it sounded good, but I'm starting to think it was all a lot of hot air."

"If you're a member of the N.S.M., you should be glad to give up your horse," said Father, baiting him. "After all, it's to help your friends, the Germans, isn't it? And when the Germans win the war, with the help of your horse, maybe they'll give you a nice big farm out in Russia somewhere."

"I don't want any stinking farm in Russia!" muttered the farmer.

Father stood up, paid the proprietor for the milk, and led the way outside.

The hour wasn't up yet, but they went to the garage anyway to see how the man was doing. They were surprised to see their car ready and waiting for them. The mechanic was washing the windshield, and he greeted them with an entirely different attitude.

"All set, sir!" he said. "That should take you a few miles now. I'm afraid those tires of yours don't have much tread left on them anymore."

"You don't know where I could pick up a couple of better ones, do you?" Father asked him.

"Well, that depends. Step into my office here a minute."

He took Father into a little cubicle, and when they returned, he shook Father's hand and hurried to open the door for them.

"By the way," he said, "you'd better check your glove compartment before you leave. I took the liberty of nosing around a little in your car. That's how I found out who I was dealing with."

Father gave him a sharp glance and quickly opened the glove compartment. He brought out a few folded newspapers.

Free Holland was the title on the front page—the secretly circulated underground paper.

"I'll be glad to take them off your hands if you're finished with them," the man offered grinning.

Father shoved them into his hands. "Thanks," he said. "You're a good man. I'll see you next week."

But when they were on their way, he asked, obviously upset, "How in the world did they get in there? Do you know, John?"

John blushed and stammered, "I-I guess I goofed, Dad. I was reading them yesterday in your studio when someone dropped in to see you. So I took them upstairs to read in my room. But Margy was cleaning there. So I went out to the garage and crawled into the car and read them in here. But then Mom called me to feed the turkeys and . . . ."

"I've got the picture," said Father. "Your absent-mindedness could have cost us all our freedom! I hope you see that. You've got to be more careful!"

Father's jovial mood had evaporated, but a few kilometers down the road, he suddenly chuckled, "Well, I guess we're all stupid once in a while, but you boys have certainly each used your share for today."

"So now it's your turn," said Fritz.

"God spare us!" said Father seriously. "These times have made me realize that if everything goes well, it's not our own doing. If I weren't sure that we are in the care of Him who rules the world, I'd have stayed home. You understand?"

He turned to look at them both. His eyes were cheerful again, and a smile played about his lips. That's what they liked about Father: he never put on an overly pious face. When he said something like that, they knew it came straight from his heart. A little later he was whistling again. Fritz leaned forward from the back seat so that his head rested between Father and John and he draped an arm around each of them. Thus they rode into the city.

The snow had stopped falling, but there was a thick layer of slush on the streets that splattered in all directions. Father drove to the local market and stopped. He looked at his watch and said, "Okay, boys! We'll meet here in about an hour, on the other side of the street. Got that?"

"Can't we go along?" asked Fritz, disappointed.

"No, I'm afraid not. I've got to see an old couple who can't stand having noisy kids around."

Again, Fritz was uncertain if Father were serious or whether he was just pulling their leg. Oh well, he sighed to himself, it just might be fun wandering around the streets of a strange city for a while. Now that the weather had improved, the streets were getting busier too. Housewives were coming out to do their shopping. People were beginning to line up in front of a butcher shop to get their ration of meat for the weekend. Others were window-shopping for clothes, which however could only be purchased after enough points had been collected on a ration card. School must have just let out here too because the sidewalks were suddenly filled with youngsters. On one corner, a man stood hawking newspapers. He approached every passer-by trying to sell a paper.

"He's peddling the Nazi newspaper, *Race and Nation*," said John guardedly. "Let's watch him and see if he sells any."

They stood by the corner of a store and studied the attitudes of people as they passed the newspaper vendor. Most of them didn't even give him a glance; they acted as if he didn't exist. Some laughed in his face, and one laborer spat at the man, just missing the newspaper held out to him. A group of school children gathered a little way off and began chanting a poem. Fritz started to join in, but John shushed him.

On the corner of the street
stands a dirty traitor!
He's a peddler of deceit,
a collaborator.
He's a Nazi — Can't you smell?—
He pollutes his station;
for a nickle he will sell
all his *Race and Nation*.

The vendor yelled at the children in anger, but they held their ground. Only when a policeman came riding down the street, did they stop their taunting and move on. They stopped again a little farther on in front of a large poster, and again they shouted with laughter.

"Come on!" said Fritz. "Let's go see what they're doing." The poster consisted of a large *V*. Underneath it were printed the words: "Victory, for Germany is winning on all fronts!" In this way the Germans tried to capitalize on the English *V* campaign and so create confusion.

One of the school children had changed *winning* to *swimming*. Then he had drawn hands on both arms of the *V*, and at the base of the *V* a caricature of Hitler's face. A wavy line representing water was drawn over Hitler's head so that he looked as if he were sinking for the last time. To one side the young artist had written, "HELP!"

Almost all the passers-by stopped to chuckle at the revised poster, but most of them looked around warily before stopping. They provided a good barometer of the prevalent mood in the city however.

Father was a little late in arriving at the agreed-upon spot. While John and Fritz were waiting, a squad of black-uniformed civil defense troops of the N.S.M. marched by. They goose-stepped just as high and stomped just as hard as their German models, and they sang their marching songs several decibels louder. No one paid them the slightest attention, except the newspaper man who stood on the curb with his arm extended in the Nazi salute.

The boys were happy when they saw the familiar little car coming down the street, for they were beginning to feel the cold. They jumped in and Father drove out of the city. Fritz heard something behind him. Sure enough! It was the gobble of turkeys.

"Didn't you sell the turkeys, Dad?" Fritz asked in surprise.

"No. Isn't that a dirty shame?" said Father. "They had already bought their birds somewhere else."

"That isn't fair!" Fritz exploded. "So you made this trip for nothing!"

"For nothing? We had a nice outing, didn't we?"

Thus they played their roles, neither one knowing for sure whether the other was also putting on or not. Darkness was beginning to fall, so Father switched on the masked headlights. John described everything they had seen in the city, from the defaced poster to the squad of Dutch Nazis.

"Watch out for those guys!" Father warned. "A few days ago they waded into a crowd and beat everyone with their belts because a few people deliberately turned their backs on them. You're better off staying out of their way. They think they own the streets."

"Don't they have to obey the law?" Fritz asked, outraged.

"They do whatever they please," replied Father. "The police may bring charges against them, but often the judge belongs to the N.S.M. too. At most, they get a small fine. Sometimes their *accusers* end up behind bars instead. I'm afraid there isn't much law left in this country any more, boys. But that won't last forever!

"Oh-oh! What's this? I thought sure those guys would stay home in this kind of weather!"

Ahead, a red light bobbed up and down as two men signaled them to stop. One wore a tightly buttoned leather coat, and the other was dressed in a police uniform. Father rolled down his window.

"Good evening, gentlemen," Father said breezily. "What can I do for you?"

"I'm with the C.C.S. sir. What are you carrying?" demanded the civilian.

"C.C.S.?" thought Fritz. "What does that stand for? Oh, of course, the Crisis Control Service. They're after black-market dealers."

"What am I carrying?" echoed Father innocently. "My two sons. That's not against the law, is it?"

"Don't you have anything in your trunk?"

"Sure, a couple turkeys. But there's no law against that either, is there?"

"Let's have a look at them," insisted the man.

"Meanwhile, let me look over your papers," said the policeman.

Father handed his wallet to the policeman. John had

to get out because the trunk of the DKW could be reached only from inside the car. The front seat had to be folded forward, and Fritz had to press himself against the back of Father's seat as he pulled forward the backrest of the rear seat, which also served as the lid to the trunk. The inspector leaned over the backrest and shone his flashlight into the trunk.

"Careful!" warned Father. "If you open it too far, those turkeys will get out, and I'll have a dickens of a time rounding them up again!"

The inspector moved his light back and forth, craning his neck to get a better look.

He ducked back outside, grinned at Father and said, "You're okay. Take good care of your cargo." And he winked.

Their papers were also in order. They were signaled to move on.

"Drive carefully. And good luck!" shouted the inspector as they drove off.

"My, that guy was unusually friendly," the boys remarked to each other as the car picked up speed. When they got home and had put the car in the garage, they found out why. Before Father could say anything, Fritz had yanked open the lid to the trunk and snapped on the dome light. The turkeys were crowded together in one corner, and they had pulled up the trunk lining. In full view lay several bundles of *Free Holland*.

They suddenly realized that they had escaped tremendous danger only because the inspector who had stopped them had been "sound." Their trip could well have had a very different ending.

"There!" exclaimed Fritz, grinning at Father. "Now you've had your turn too."

It took Father a little while to recover. He heaved a deep, quavering sigh.

"We can be extremely thankful," he said. "You see what I meant. You can never be too careful. From now on I'll have to fasten that lining at all four corners. Well, now you know, Fritz. But I can count on you to keep mum, right? Like the three monkeys: you've seen nothing, heard nothing, and you'll say nothing. Got that?"

"Of course, Dad!" Fritz assured him.

"Let's shake on that."

Fritz shook hands solemnly. As he looked into Father's face, he realized he would never find a better friend in the whole world. It had often bothered him that Father and John discussed things he wasn't permitted to know. Now he was in on it too. Now he was being treated like a man. And, like a man, he helped to unload the car. The turkeys were put back in the pen with the others, and Uncle Gerrit took the bundles of newspapers and disappeared into the darkness. Fritz didn't ask where he was taking them; he thought of the three monkeys.

Mother stood waiting at the door. By her hug, Fritz guessed that she too wasn't entirely ignorant of what was going on.

After supper, Fritz again went for a ride with Father. This time, however, he wasn't sitting on the edge of his seat in anticipation.

Mr. Wiesel opened the door when they arrived and

hurried them inside, for the light from within shone out through the open door, and the blackout was strictly enforced.

Mr. Wiesel ushered them into the living room and as soon as they were inside, Fritz gathered up his courage and began his apology. But his teacher must have sensed that Fritz was genuinely penitent, for he didn't let Fritz finish! He put his hand on Fritz's shoulder and said, "Never mind, my boy. I understand. Sometimes this blasted war makes puppets of us all. It drives everyone a little crazy at times. But let's try not to make life unbearable for each other."

Mr. Wiesel sighed wearily and passed his hand over his forehead, as if he were trying to erase something from his mind.

"I'd like to talk to you alone, Mr. Wiesel, if you don't mind," said Father.

"All right," nodded Mr. Wiesel. "Fritz, you can join my wife in the family room."

Fritz sat with Mrs. Wiesel for almost an hour without getting bored. The room was cozy, and Mrs. Wiesel kept pouring tea and showing him dozens of pictures of Italy and Switzerland. She told of the trips she and her husband had made, and she managed to make it sound extremely fascinating. Fritz was almost sorry when the sliding door opened and Father entered, followed by Mr. Wiesel. Father shook hands with the Wiesels and said good night.

"You stop in again, sometime soon," Mrs. Wiesel told Fritz. To which he nodded eagerly.

In the car Father said, "It was just as I suspected. Except, the English concentration camp was even worse than I had heard! Mr. Wiesel's mother entered the camp with three children. She left with only one. Now do you understand why he's the way he is? Do me a favor, Fritz. If any of your buddies gives him a hard time, set him straight. Give him a clout on the ear if you have to. And don't you dare call Mr. Wiesel a traitor ever again! He admits he was fooled for a while, but I guarantee that pretty soon he'll be behind us a hundred percent! Yesterday, he told me, he saw a Jew being kicked out of a store by a couple of Nazis.''

CHAPTER FOUR

About two weeks later, on a summery April afternoon, a tall, skinny student rang the doorbell of the De
Boer house. When John answered the door, the young
man asked if he could speak to "Mr. De Boer, Mr.
Everett De Boer." He said he had just arrived by train.

Father wasn't home, but when John passed this information on to the young man, and saw the look of intense disappointment cross his haggard face, he didn't
have the heart to turn him away. So John invited him in
and asked him to wait in the studio until Father got
home. John led him into the studio to a chair by the
window, and then left him alone for a few minutes to
tell his mother about their guest and to ask her to make
him a cup of tea. When he returned, the fellow had
moved to a chair in the darkest corner of the room.
There he sat, fidgeting, and when John gave him the
makings for a cigarette, he saw that the man's hands

trembled so violently he could hardly get it rolled.

John made small talk about the beautiful weather and about the trains, which were always so crowded lately. The young man told John that he was from Amsterdam, but that he wasn't planning to return that day. Then the conversation lapsed, and John didn't know what else to say. There was something strange about this visitor that made John uneasy. He acted spooked, furtive; as if he were afraid to be there. And he smoked his cigarette much too fast. His hair, too, looked strange. It was much too black for the unusually pale face. If he hadn't had such a friendly face and honest eyes you would have thought something was bothering his conscience.

Suddenly Harry Hoeks, the next-door neighbor, passed by the window and the young man jerked back into the shadows. In a terrified voice he asked, "Who's that?"

"That?" asked John. "Oh, that's just our neighbor. I guess he's going out back to talk to the gardener."

"Oh, sure!" said the young man, laughing nervously. "Of course. You see, well . . . I thought . . . ."

Just then Mother entered, carrying a cup of tea. She shook hands with the thin young man, and he introduced himself as "Overbeek, Max Overbeek from Amsterdam." Then he sat down again and stirred his tea in silence. But Mother could always be counted upon to put strangers at ease, and this time was no exception. With kindly concern she asked about his trip and his job and then about his parents.

Max told them he was a medical student in Amsterdam, where he lived in a boarding house. His mother and father lived in Indonesia, but he hadn't heard from them for almost two years. As he was talking about his mother, tears came into his eyes, and suddenly he grabbed Mother's hand and sobbed, "Oh, please, Ma'am, you've got to help me!"

Then his whole story came spilling out. During the first year of the war, he had simply carried on with his medical studies as usual. But during the general strike in February of last year, he had seen hundreds of Jews herded away like cattle, and he had begun to hate the Nazis. As a result, he and a couple of friends had become involved in resistance work: spreading illegal literature and pictures of the royal family, and carrying messages to be relayed to England.

For the past two months they had been hiding two English fliers who had been shot down at night and had parachuted to safety. He had been trying to help them get back to England, and he too had wanted to go to England so that he could fight with the Allies to help free his parents. Three of his friends had planned to go along. They had made contact with a man in a coastal village, who could help them get hold of a motorboat, or at least, that was what he had promised.

The man—De Raaf was his name—had met with them a few times: once in Max's room; and he had come to know the whole group. One of Max's teachers had advised them against the project—Mr. . . . no, he had better not mention his name. But they had persisted, putting all their trust in De Raaf.

Two weeks ago they had gotten the signal! Everything

was set; they could leave immediately. That afternoon, they and the English fliers were supposed to go to a specified address at the west end of the city, where they would get their final instructions. There, too, a car would be waiting for them to take them to their boat.

He had arrived late. A friend, one he didn't wholly trust, had held him up. But this delay saved him, for when he approached the address, an S.S. truck was already parked in front of the door. From a cafe across the street, where he took refuge, he watched his friends and the two fliers being led outside, their hands tied behind them. They were hammered into the truck by S.S. rifle butts.

De Raaf, the man who was supposed to be helping them, emerged some time later, after the spectators had dispersed. He was with a German officer. They stood together on the curb for a few minutes, laughing and talking. Then they went their separate ways. The dirty swine!

Not until it was dark did he dare go out into the street again. First, he went and warned his old teacher, who had been in on the planning. With their brutal interrogations the S.S. might force his buddies to name others. He didn't dare go back to his boarding house, so he went to the friend who had delayed him that afternoon. He had to share his grief with someone, so he took this classmate into his confidence.

The friend let him stay the night, but he was afraid to hide him longer. So the next day he was forced to find another place to stay. He concocted a story about how he had gotten into trouble with his landlady playing sick

in order to cut classes, and the parents of one of his other classmates put him up. But two days later, they found out what had really happened, for the Germans had come looking for him at his boarding house, and the news spread quickly among his fellow students. Then, after dyeing his hair so he wouldn't be recognized, he moved to another address. Two weeks later, however, his former teacher came to warn him that his description and picture had appeared in a police bulletin, and he was being sought as a criminal.

Any policeman might pick him up and turn him over to the Germans. The best thing for him to do, his old friend advised him, was to get out of Amsterdam as soon as possible. And then he had given Max the De Boers's address and arranged a ride for him to Amersfoort. He had traveled the rest of the way by train.

His old teacher had also given him a note. He had it with him. Here it was. He sure hoped they could take him in, because if they didn't, he had no idea where to go next. Then he might as well turn himself in to the Germans.

"I sure hope you can help me!" the young man said. "I don't know what else to do." His voice broke and his breath came in quavering sobs. He apologized, but, he said, his nerves were shot from constant tension and fear.

Mother walked over to the sobbing student and hugged his head against her breast as if he were her own son.

"Don't worry, my boy," she assured him. "We'll take care of you, you can be sure of that. There's no need to be afraid anymore. You're a long way from Amsterdam now. Here, you've let your tea get cold. I'll fetch you another cup. How about a National Socialist cookie? See, it looks delicious, but when you bite into it, you break your teeth."

He laughed through his tears, and with a strangled voice, he said, "I'd like to bite all their heads off, even if it did cost me my teeth. The dirty swine!"

"Well, so would I," said Mother, "but I'm afraid they'd give you a bad case of indigestion. Say, John, couldn't you go and get Father? You know where he is, don't you?"

Yes, John knew where Father was. A secret meeting was being held at the pastor's house. The meeting had been called to plan counter-measures against the German proscription of young men. When the boys reached draft age, they were supposed to turn themselves in to be sent to big camps, where, so the party line went, they would learn to be men and work hard. Actually, the purpose of the camps was to indoctrinate them with the ideas of National Socialism. This program had to be fought every way possible, said Father.

As he pedaled toward the parsonage, John thought about the student waiting in the studio. The young man had endured a lot; he seemed awfully frightened and nervous. When he had knocked on the door, he had reminded John of a scared rabbit. Had this same fellow been the leader of a group of young men who were going to take two fliers back to England? It seemed incredible!

On the way back home, John filled Father in on everything that had happened. When they got to the house, the young man had calmed down considerably. He paled again, however, when Father sat down in front of him and began firing questions. What was his complete name, where was he born, what was his mother's name, his grandfather's, where had his parents lived in Indonesia, what was the name of the street, what were the names of his professors in Amsterdam, and so on.

Suddenly John realized what Father was doing: he had to make sure that this boy wasn't a spy sent by the Germans. Well, Father could put his mind at ease. Max Overbeek answered quickly, without stumbling. You had only to look into his eyes to see that he wasn't a traitor.

"Let me see your letter," said Father, and the young man took the note out of his pocket. It consisted of a few lines scribbled on a page torn out of a small notebook. Father put it down on his desk, without indicating whether he recognized the handwriting.

"How did you get here?" he asked the young man.

"I took the train to Groningen and then a bus the rest of the way."

"Did you pass through any checks on the way?"

"No, sir. Fortunately I didn't."

"Did you ask anyone for directions?"

"Yes, sir. The bus driver."

"Hmmm, were there many people on the bus?"

"Yes, sir. It was full. The driver didn't know where you lived, but the man sitting next to me overheard my question, and he told me how to get here. That was stupid of me, wasn't it—to ask for directions here?"

"Let me see your identification."

With a trembling hand, the youth pulled his wallet out of his pocket. Before he could take out his identification, Father took the wallet out of his hands and browsed through it. Then he studied the I.D. card, turning it over and over.

"Have you been messing with this?" Father asked him.

"Yes, I-I tried to change my name."

Father shook his head.

"This way it's worse than before. You'd have been picked up at the first check. You can thank God you got as far as you did. Also, because of that funny hair—when did you dye it?"

"About two weeks ago."

"You should have dyed it again. Your red roots are showing, I can see them from here. Were you wearing a cap on the bus?"

"Yes, sir."

"Tell me, what would you have said about this letter if you'd been picked up?"

"Letter?"

"This letter from Mr. Coenen. It asks me to help you. A good thing it doesn't have my name or address on it."

"Oh, don't worry, they'd never have gotten their hands on that!" he said confidently. "I'd have thrown it away, or eaten it, if necessary."

"And if they had asked you where you were going, what then?"

"I guess I never really thought about that. I don't know . . . ."

"You *should* have thought about it," Father said

severely. "You should have had your answer ready, so that you could have replied without hesitating."

"But I'd never have given them your name, sir!" exclaimed the young man.

"Oh no?" said Father. "Are you *sure*? Do you know what the Gestapo does to make someone talk?"

"Yes, sir. I know! They torture you in all kinds of ways. And when I think of my buddies . . . ! But honest, sir, I wouldn't have told them your name. At least, I hope I'd have the guts to keep my mouth shut."

"That sounds a little better," said Father. "Now if you'll wait here a minute—we'll talk a little more later."

He motioned John to follow him, and led Mother and John into the bedroom. He sighed, looked at them both, and asked, "Well, what do you think? What are we going to do with our medical student?"

"You mean you still have to ask!" expostulated Mother. "That poor boy! Of course he's going to stay here! You can't put him back out in the street."

Father laughed.

"You women!" he said. "What were you saying just yesterday? 'Stop fooling with all that illegal literature,' you said, 'and with all the rest of it too. Get out of the resistance altogether, because I can't sleep nights!' And now you want to take in somebody who's on the German's most-wanted list. This is much more dangerous!"

"But this is completely different," argued Mother. "What was it you read from the Bible a few days ago? It was in Isaiah. 'Hide the outcast; don't betray the fugitive.' What could be clearer? Nowhere does it say you should risk your life peddling illegal newspapers."

"No, but it does tell us to oppose the lie."

"I still say it's different," Mother maintained. "This concerns a human being who's in need. That poor boy! He has no father or mother to turn to. It's our duty to take care of him—he's been sent to us! What would they do to him if they caught him?"

"They'd kill him."

Mother stared at him shocked. "Then that settles it! Such a fine boy—he's hardly a man yet. Those thugs! Those murderers! They wouldn't dare touch him here, they'd have to deal with me first. As long as I'm here, they'll not get their hands on him."

She was flushed with outrage, and tears of anger had sprung to her eyes. Father put his arms about her.

"You're a fine woman—every inch a mother!" he told her. "And I feel just as you do, honey. We have no other choice. It's our God-given duty. I do trust the boy; he seems completely honest. But he's done some pretty stupid things. Anyway, now we'll have to make plans. John, will you ask Uncle Gerrit to join us? He's usually full of ideas."

In the presence of the old man, who was given a quick resumé of what was going on, Father informed the youth that he could stay. His joy was so evident that Uncle Gerrit took to him at once. They decided that Max should live in the camper parked behind the garage after it was moved into the woods behind the orchard. That way, if he were traced and the Germans came to search the house, they would find nothing. Father accepted the job of getting him a new I.D. card. He would use the picture from the old one.

"We'll pass you off as my nephew, okay?" said Father. "You're a son of my brother in Indonesia. From now on your name is William De Boer, and my wife and I will be your uncle and aunt. You were born in Bandung, right? That will stay the same. But your place of residence should be changed. What other cities besides Amsterdam do you know well?"

"Rotterdam. I lived there for a year with my parents, when they were here on furlough."

"Good. Then your place of residence will be Rotterdam. How would you like to be a teacher? You think you could handle that as an occupation? Your story is that you're here temporarily on sick leave. You've had a nervous breakdown. That's not far from the truth, is it?

"Now you've got to spend some time imagining yourself into your new identity. For example, you should have the name of your school, its location, and the names of your colleagues and principal right at the tip of your tongue. You should also be able to produce a letter granting you a leave of absence. We should be able to get hold of one of those.

"Above all, dear nephew, remember this: You are to follow to the letter all the rules we lay down, and you've got to be careful every minute of the day! You got that? Remember, from now on, any blunder won't only endanger you, but us as well. Can I count on you?"

"Of course, sir. Ah, I mean, Uncle."

"Everett," said Father. "Just call me Uncle Everett."

"You can count on me, Uncle Everett. I won't cause you any trouble," promised William De Boer.

"We've got to do something about that hair right away," said Uncle Gerrit, frowning.

"You're right," agreed Father. "But we can hardly take him to the barber."

"The barber?" grinned Uncle Gerrit. "For such an ugly thatch? No self-respecting barber would touch it. But I've sheared quite a few sheep in my day, so William here should be a cinch. Come on, follow me to the shed, my little black sheep. We'll see if you can give us three bags full."

A few minutes later Father was driving off, and Uncle Gerrit was filling the air with quips and snips. He hadn't gone very far before he was heading back to the house for another pair of scissors. "That kid has hair like copper wire!" he said.

When he returned, the new addition to the De Boer family was slouched forward on the crate that served as a barber chair—fast asleep. When Uncle Gerrit shook him awake to finish the haircut, Max explained that he hadn't been able to sleep a wink the last couple of nights.

"Well, tonight you should sleep like a baby—seeing's how you were just reborn," joked Uncle Gerrit. "Now hold your head still, or I'll take off your ears. Maybe that wouldn't be a bad idea! Then no one would recognize you for sure."

But Uncle Gerrit spared Max's ears; the haircut turned out to be enough. John fetched a mirror and held it in front of his newborn and newshorn cousin. He now had a deep-red brush cut, and although Uncle Gerrit's scissors had slipped here and there, he didn't look too bad. William De Boer frowned at his new identity in the mirror.

"How do you do, Mr. De Boer," he greeted himself.

"Such airs!" said Uncle Gerrit. "Mr. De Boer, my foot! You look more like an ex-con than a Mr. Anybody. You'd better wear your cap, or you'll scare everyone to death. And you'll catch your death of cold besides. Now you'd better sweep up your three bags of wool, my little black sheep, and then bury it out in the garden. Here's a shovel. Make sure you get it all. But hustle! We've got to fix you a place to sleep before nightfall.

"Ah, here's our dear little Fritz! He always shows up just when we need him. Right Fritz? Come here, my boy! Let me introduce you to your cousin from Indonesia. Come on, say something. Tell him you're glad to meet him!"

When the strange young man told him that his name was William De Boer, the son of Uncle Nick and Aunt Vera in Indonesia, Fritz swallowed it hook, line, and sinker—at least, at first. But when he saw the red-headed young man sweeping up black hair, he began asking questions; and he wasn't satisfied until he had heard the whole story.

Fritz thought it was great! Now they had their own "diver," as those who went into hiding from the Germans were called. And he enthusiastically helped push the camper through the orchard and into the woods. Father had picked up the camper several weeks ago. It had been owned by a landscape painter who had been living in a house on the seashore, but who had been evicted by the Germans to make room for coastal defenses.

Before the war, the painter had taken the camper along on his sketching trips. It had been in Rome and in the Alps. Now it was parked in some woods on a neglected piece of farmland. Tricia came carrying blankets and a pillow to make her new cousin's bed. She had never before seen the young man, but she too was overjoyed that they were helping him.

After Mother fed him, he crawled into the camper for an afternoon nap and would have slept all day if Uncle Gerrit hadn't awakened him. It was almost supper time, so he ate first, and then Uncle Gerrit put him to work stacking branches up against the camper.

By nightfall, the camper was completely hidden. The door was concealed by the branches of a large fir tree. At the back of the camper a small burrow had been left open, and Uncle Gerrit had sawed a trap door in the floor of the camper. That way, if any unwelcome guests came to the door, William could slip out through the trap door.

Surrounded as it was by branches, the camper was as dark as a cave inside. "You don't need light anyway," said Uncle Gerrit. "Whenever you sit down, you fall asleep. You don't need light when you're sleeping." But the next day, Uncle Gerrit showed up at the camper with an old kerosene lamp. He'd sweet-talked a farmer out of it, he said.

William didn't use the old lamp very much, however, for he spent most of his evenings as part of the De Boer family circle. He soon won the heart of the entire family with his friendly, easy-going manner; and after he had gotten over his anxiety, he was full of stories and jokes. Most of them he had picked up from the students in Amsterdam.

"Hey, Fritz! Here's a good riddle for you. What's the difference between the primitive German and the modern German? Can't you guess . . . ? The primitive Germans were humans dressed in animal skins, and the modern Germans are animals dressed in human skins."

Before Fritz had stopped laughing, William was telling another story. One day in Amsterdam a squad of Dutch Nazis had marched by, dressed in their black uniforms. On the sidewalk stood an old man, who shouted, "Hi there, Jim; Joe! How's it going, Paul!"

One of his friends who was with him asked suspiciously, "How come you know so many of those Nazis?"

"What?" the old man said. "Can't you guess? Don't forget, I've been the warden of the local prison here most of my life!"

The next day, Fritz and John repeated all the stories to their classmates, and soon they were being told all over the city. The boys were careful not to mention their source. Even the two youngest girls, Hanneke and Trudy, had been drilled not to talk about their Indonesian cousin. It was amazing to see how well they kept their secret. Perhaps, in this time of great danger, they understood more than the grown-ups gave them credit for.

Once, when Hanneke brought home a girlfriend after school, William was out in the orchard helping Uncle Gerrit. The girlfriend asked, "Who's that? Are you guys hiding a diver too?"

"A diver?" Hanneke replied innocently. "Oh, that's no diver. That's my cousin from Rotterdam."

"You never told me you had a cousin visiting you."

That's because he only just got here," fibbed Hanneke. "He's a school teacher, but he can't teach because he gets these awful headaches because of all the bombs that fell on Rotterdam."

The last part she made up herself. She remembered the dreadful bombing at the beginning of the war, when she had been visiting her aunts in Rotterdam. Even now, two years later, she was sometimes wakened during the night by the drone of English bombers heading for Hamburg or Bremen, and then she would scream in panic for Mother.

But now they didn't have to keep William's presence such a strict secret any more, for that too could raise suspicion. William had new identification papers, and from a doctor in Rotterdam he had a letter prescribing a six-month leave of absence for nervous tension. Father didn't say how he had gotten hold of these papers, of course, but he assured William he'd have no trouble getting through a check with them.

William even started going along to church. There were other divers who surfaced for Sunday worship—the pastor himself was hiding two of them. Soon William even got up the nerve to go into town by himself. Mother didn't approve of this at all, for she would have liked to keep him in the house all day where she was sure he was safe. Sometimes Father teased her about trying to make a mama's boy out of her adopted nephew; he said that she fussed over William more than over her own boys. But Mother paid no attention. She saw to it that the thin young man who had come to their door put on six pounds in the first two weeks.

One evening they were sitting together in the living room, when Father read an article from the local newspaper which reported that seventy-two men had been shot to death by the Germans for acts against the occupation government. Mother looked at William, jumped up, and gathered him into her arms, weeping.

The news also made a deep impression on the rest of the family, for among the executed men were several whom they knew very well. One was Mr. Van Vliet, who had been at the house many times to pick up weapons that Father had collected. Occasionally, he had stayed overnight. He had worked for a secret organization called the O.D., an armed police force that was getting ready to take over at the breakdown of German rule.

All the other men who had been executed were friends and co-workers of Van Vliet, most of them ex-officers. Had they underestimated the cunning of the Nazis? Soon rumors were flying that they had kept lists of all those who had helped them and that these lists had fallen into German hands.

A few days later, Radio Orange urged everyone to keep a close watch on their tongues about things that might interest the enemy. People were much too eager to pass on the latest tidbit of information, without asking themselves whether their loose tongues might endanger someone else's life.

Sometimes, however, even silence was not enough.

People even had to be ready to feed the Nazis false information. Uncle Gerrit, for example, was playing a game of cat and mouse with one of their neighbors, Mr. Wallinga, for he was not only a Nazi collaborator, but he was also a man who liked to harm others.

There were other people in town who were Nazis—who belonged to the N.S.M. because this party had promised the farmers a pot of gold at the end of the Nazi rainbow. But they would never think of betraying their neighbors. With Wallinga, however, you had to be on your guard every minute, so everyone tried to steer clear of the man. He had quarreled with almost everyone in town, and he was despised and hated by them all.

Father had already crossed swords with him at the beginning of the war, for the fellow had insulted the Queen in Father's presence.

"As far as I'm concerned," he had snarled, "that bitch can stay where she is!"

Since then, they passed on the street without greeting each other. Father wasn't one to put on a false front, but Uncle Gerrit didn't think that was wise, so he tried to patch things up by pretending that he too was a Nazi sympathizer. Happily, Wallinga was so dense that he believed almost everything Uncle Gerrit told him, and the latter gradually won his trust.

One day last January, two strangers had knocked on Wallinga's door and, speaking with a strange accent, they had asked for food. But Wallinga wasn't about to help anyone, and as they turned to go, he had seen the letters *K.G.* on the back of their jackets. Despite his stupidity, he happened to know that those letters were the German equivalent of P.O.W.—prisoner of war. And he had hurried into town to report them to the police. The latter had no choice but to arrest the fugitives, and the next day they were shipped back to Germany.

The whole county soon knew that Wallinga was to blame for sending the starving escapees back to a German prison camp, and he was denounced everywhere. However, when Uncle Gerrit ran into Wallinga next day as he was fixing the fence, he congratulated him and told him that he had done a great deed.

"Who knows?" Uncle Gerrit went on. "Those guys probably got a good look at everything when they were in Germany, and they would have taken all that information straight to the English. Haven't you ever asked yourself how it is that the English planes can find those German cities in the dark of night? Well, now you know! By turning those guys in, you've probably saved hundreds of German women and children."

Although he didn't exactly follow Gerrit's reasoning, Wallinga glowed with pride. Finally, he thought, here was someone who could recognize and appreciate his true worth.

"It was hard work, too!" he explained, hungry for more praise. "It was so slippery out, I could hardly keep my footing. And it's no small distance from my place to town! Besides, the first cop wasn't home, so I had to go all the way to the other guy's house!"

"Man oh man!" exclaimed Uncle Gerrit. "And at your age! I'll tell you what. Next time something like

that happens, you call me. The De Boers have a
telephone. You give me the message, and I'll call it in to
the police. That's a lot easier. And if the phone isn't
working, I'll send one of the boys into town with a
sealed letter. That would save you a long trip. My boss
won't mind."

"Well . . . ," said Wallinga doubtfully.

"I mean it!" Uncle Gerrit assured him. "You've got
him all wrong—just because you've had a couple of run-
ins with him. He isn't such a bad guy. Really! He's
beginning to see that if we're ever going to have better
times, Germany has to win the war. He just hasn't got
the guts to come out and say so, like you!"

He hoped the rancorous old Nazi believed him; for it
would make things less dangerous for the De Boers.
Sure enough, a month later Wallinga sought out Uncle
Gerrit in the garden and told him that he had seen a
stranger at the Hoving farm. If it wasn't another one of
those P.O.W.'s, then it had to be a diver, he said. And
would Uncle Gerrit call the police for him, because it
was much too cold for him to walk to town. Of course,
Uncle Gerrit said he was only too happy to make the
call, and he did—but only after Father had rushed over
to the Hoving farm to warn the people.

An hour later, two policemen stopped at Wallinga's
house, two sound men, Uncle Gerrit had seen to that.
First, they thoroughly interrogated him, and then
demanded that he come along to show them the exact
spot where he had seen the stranger. They left him standing outside in the cold while they searched the house
and all the buildings on the Hoving farm. The

policemen took their time and just couldn't resist Mrs. Hoving's coffee.

All this time, Wallinga stood outside shivering in the freezing wind. When they finally came back outside, the two policemen lit into him and accused him of leading them on a wild goose chase, for, of course, the diver was long gone. If he ever made fools of them again, they warned him, they would make him wish he had never opened his mouth. Even if he did belong to the N.S.M. that didn't give him a license to trifle with the police!

Uncle Gerrit didn't see hide nor hair of Wallinga for three days. Then he came to Uncle Gerrit to complain about how he had been treated by the police. "Everybody makes a mistake once in a while," he said bitterly.

"Next time," he said to Uncle Gerrit, "don't bother calling them cops. We'll go straight to the Germans!"

"Good idea!" said Uncle Gerrit. "I think you're right."

One afternoon in May, Uncle Gerrit was out digging in the garden with William, when Wallinga came shuffling over, eyeing William with undisguised curiosity.

"Hunn!" he snorted, nodding contemptuously in William's direction. "He's not much help, is he?"

"What do you expect, man?" agreed Uncle Gerrit, jovially. "What do school teachers know about anything? All they can do is give the kids a hard time. Working here will do him good. We'll teach him a few things!"

"Oh, he's a school teacher, is he?" pried Wallinga, talking about William as if he were a child who couldn't speak for himself.

"Yep," said Uncle Gerrit. "You didn't think we'd give room and board to a P.O.W. or a diver did you? We're not crazy! He's the boss's nephew, and he teaches in Rotterdam."

"Where?" asked the old turncoat, who was a little hard of hearing.

"In Rotterdam."

"But what's he doing *here*? It isn't summer vacation yet."

"I'll tell you, man. It's a sad story," began Uncle Gerrit. Then, turning to William he said, "You don't mind if I tell him, do you William? Wallinga here is a good friend of mine. He'll understand.

"Listen Wallinga, you've heard how the English bombed the blazes out of Rotterdam and then blamed it on the Germans? Well, William here was right in the middle of it! It's a miracle that he survived! And now his nerves are shot. He looks okay now, but you should hear him at night. No wonder, though! Just imagine, Wallinga, if the English started dropping bombs on your farm tonight. Your wife dead, your daughter burnt to a crisp!"

"You're right, it'd be awful!" said Wallinga with a shudder.

"Your horses, all your cows. Blown to smithereens!" Uncle Gerrit went on.

"Horrible! How horrible!" cried Wallinga, as if this were even worse.

"Your helper killed, and you dead as a doornail too! That would drive you bananas, too, wouldn't it?"

Wallinga nodded gravely, deeply impressed. Suddenly a strange, strangling sound came from William, and he buried his face in his handkerchief. He quickly walked away to the other end of the garden, where he stood looking out across the fields with his back to the two men.

"I guess we'd better not talk about it any more," said Uncle Gerrit in a low voice. "See? It's got him all upset. Did you hear those planes again last night? What a ruckus, hey? Can you sleep through all that?"

"I laid in bed cursing the devils," Wallinga spat out. "They don't dare show themselves during the day, those yellow limeys!"

"You can say that again! I'll bet they do a lot of damage, too. There ought to be a law against it, my boss was saying the other day."

"I heard that they toss out pictures and stuff that burst into flame when you take them home!" said the old farmer indignantly.

"They'll get what's coming to them!" predicted Uncle Gerrit. "My boss says that once Hitler's in England, the war won't last long anymore."

"Your boss said that?" blurted Wallinga. "He's really coming around, isn't he?" He laughed in self-satisfaction. "Yesterday I was talking to another guy just like him. First, he didn't have a good word for the Germans either, but now that they're beating the stuffings out of the Russians and taking over Africa, he wants to join the N.S.M. too. Just wait and see! In another year they'll *all* be following in our footsteps!"

"Sure as shooting!" Uncle Gerrit chimed in. "With

their hats in their hands and their tails between their legs!"

"Every one of them!" crowed the old farmer triumphantly.

William, who had moved back within earshot, once again uttered a strange, muffled moan and staggered off with his hands to his face.

"Look at him, the poor guy! He's having another fit," said Uncle Gerrit. To William, he called out, "What's the matter Willy, my boy? Is that head of yours bothering you again? Why don't you go up to the house to your auntie? She'll put a cold washcloth on your forehead.

"See? He just can't take it! We shouldn't have talked about all those awful things. I'd better go with him and see that he's all right. When he's like this, he might even take a notion to jump into the canal."

He found William in the shed, weeping with laughter as he related Uncle Gerrit's conversation to Father.

"That guy," chortled William, clutching his sides, "is as stupid as a horse's behind!"

"Oh, I don't know," protested Uncle Gerrit. "If he were *that* smart, I wouldn't dare lead him on that way."

"When Hitler's in England," William went on. "You meant safely behind bars. And the hats and tails—were those for his funeral? Ha-ha! Wallinga was beaming as if he could see himself at the head of the parade."

"Maybe so," said Father. "But let's not forget that Hitler is far from buried!"

"You're right," Uncle Gerrit agreed soberly. "And that Wallinga is dangerous, precisely because he *is* so stupid. Anybody with any brains would think twice before betraying his neighbors. He'd weigh the consequences, but not Wallinga. As soon as he sees something fishy he goes running to the Germans. So why don't you try to get on his good side, Everett? Next time you see him, say hello."

"Nuts to that!" exploded Father. "I'll be drawn and quartered before I shine up to such scum!"

"Now you're talking like a horse's behind yourself," said Uncle Gerrit. "I can see the hate in your eyes, and when a person acts out of hate, he's usually wrong. Let me remind you of your own words: 'You're not supposed to hate people, only evil!' Just think it over, Everett."

He talked to Father as he had done when Father was still a little boy and Gerrit was working for Father's father. As he finished, he turned and started back toward the garden.

"I can't play games with him like you do," Father called after him angrily. "To me things are far too serious for that!"

Uncle Gerrit stopped and slowly came back. He looked at Father with a mixture of sadness and anger.

"Do you really think this is just a game for me, Everett? Then you don't know me very well. You think it doesn't make me sick to put on a false front like that? Sometimes I'd like to bash the man's head in! And maybe one day it'll come to that.

"But for the time being, I try to pull his fangs by deceit and a friendly face. And if sticking up my arm and shouting 'Huzzah!' will help, then I'll do that too.

Yes, I'll lie and dissemble, Everett, but only to serve the truth. Remember that! And I'm not afraid to ask for God's blessing on my 'little games.'

"No, just keep your mouth shut for a minute!" he snapped, as Father tried to interrupt him. "Just let me finish. This war isn't over yet, not by a long shot. And I shudder to think what still lies ahead of us. All that work you're doing for the underground—that's great! Keep it up! But you've also got to think of your family.

"Here!" He picked up little Hansie, who had come toddling over to them, and handed him to Father. "Think of him. And if you can't do it for yourself, then swallow your pride for him. It's for him and for Hanneke and Fritz and all of you that I lie and play my games!" Now his lips were beginning to tremble, he quickly turned and stomped away. "Be as harmless as doves and as cunning as snakes," they heard him mutter.

"Uncle Gerrit!" shouted Father, but the old man stalked on as if he didn't hear him.

Then Father ran after him and grabbed him by the arm.

"Uncle Gerrit, you ornery old cuss! Remember how you used to box my ears when I was a kid? Well, I guess I've got one coming right now. Come on, right here!"

They both had tears in their eyes, and when they looked at each other, they grabbed hold of each other and wrestled playfully like two young boys. And Father ended up getting his ears boxed.

"You'd better stay around the house the rest of the day." Father called to William, as he stood rubbing his ears.

That afternoon Father worked side by side with Uncle Gerrit, planting beans in the garden.

CHAPTER FIVE

That day John and Tricia came home from school an hour later than usual, and Fritz hadn't showed up yet by suppertime. Something unusual was going on in town, said John. The place was in a turmoil! That morning hundreds of men had begun arriving in town by train, and in small groups they had made their way to the old army base, chatting and joking. They were all ex-officers who had been taken prisoner by the Germans in 1940, but who had later been freed along with the rest of the army.

They had been ordered to report to their base today. The Germans had done this before. After checking everyone's papers, they had sent the men home again. It was just a formality. Extra trains had been scheduled for their return trip, and they were assured that their travel expenses would be paid. So they had no reason to be suspicious, and they had come to the base as if gathering for a reunion.

But when they were all there, so went the story, German soldiers armed with rifles and submachine guns had suddenly appeared at the windows and doors. The shocked men were told that they were under arrest and would all be shipped to Germany. They had not respected the magnanimity of the Fuehrer, who had freed them on their word of honor, and they had become involved in activities directed against the occupation government.

When John and Tricia came home, the ex-officers were still locked in the base barracks, but people had bagun gathering along the streets that led to the railway station. They expected the men to be put on the train for Germany that same evening. No wonder Fritz wasn't home! He had to be right on top of everything, of course.

Father and John and Uncle Gerrit drove into town to find him. They arrived just in time. As they neared the station, people were crowding both sides of the road, standing even in the hedges. Between them, guarded on both sides by heavily armed German soldiers, marched the Dutch officers in orderly ranks. They marched proudly, giving no hint of the emotions that must have been tearing at their hearts. They knew in all likelihood they'd not see their wives and families for the rest of the war, and possibly never again. Despite the heavy guard the people along the roads shouted all kinds of "treasonous" encouragement to the men:

"Hang in there guys!"

"It won't be long."

"Pretty soon the shoe will be on the other foot!"

"You'll be back!"

"Oso, men! Oso!"

The men smiled and nodded and gratefully caught the small parcels of food that were tossed to them by the waiting people. One civilian pulled off his coat and quickly handed it to one of the officers who had come without one. In doing so, he inadvertently bumped one of the German soldiers, but the guard did nothing. Was he perhaps ashamed of the way they had tricked these men? All along the route, notes and letters fluttered to the street under the feet of the marchers. After they had passed by, people hurried to pick them up. For many of the officers, this was their final message to their families.

The railway station was cordoned off by German soldiers so that no one could follow the men to the station. The officers marched onto the platform and into the waiting train. Then, suddenly, from the loaded train came the sound of the national anthem. The Germans dashed about shouting and screaming orders. Some even fired into the air.

But to no avail, for the words carried far into the dusk of the summer evening, filled with the fearless resolve of hundreds of strong male voices. And the people thronging around the station joined in. As the train pulled out, they sang:

> My shield and my defender
> Art Thou, O Lord, my God . . . .

They watched the train disappear down the tracks. Then

the police moved in, urging everyone to go home, and the crowd dispersed, many weeping.

John, Father and Uncle Gerrit still hadn't seen Fritz. As they walked back down the street away from the station, they suddenly saw Fritz and one of his friends chasing an older boy. They caught up to the boy, knocked him down, and began to pound on him wherever they found an opening. But then Father was on top of them and grabbed Fritz by the collar.

"Aren't you ashamed of yourself?" Father scolded. "Come along! We'll talk when we get home."

But Fritz was shaking with fury. He almost broke loose and attacked the older boy again.

"That dirty Nazi! I'll kill him! You know what he did? He picked up a whole bunch of letters, and he was ripping them up! That filthy rat! I should have kicked his teeth in!"

Suddenly he seemed to forget all about the other boy, and he turned to Father. "But I got them all, Dad! We got all the pieces, and I'll glue them all back together. And then I can mail them, okay, Dad? Those officers are counting on it! I bet I got more than thirty of them! My pockets are jammed!"

On the way home, Fritz talked nonstop about everything he'd heard and seen that day. He was convinced that the English invasion was due any day. He had heard it from several people who said that the Germans had rounded up all the officers so that when the Allies arrived, the people would have no leaders and wouldn't be able to help their liberators. The landing craft loaded with Allied soldiers, would come roaring up

on the beaches by the hundreds! This month! Because
May was the quietest month of the year on the English
Channel.

Fritz and the others worked until late that night
piecing the letters together. Father called up some of the
wives who could be reached by telephone, and he told
them that their husbands' letters would be arriving
soon. Then they went to bed to the drone of English
planes passing over on their way to bomb Germany.
Tonight, especially, it was music to their ears.

In the days that followed, Fritz could think of nothing
but the next radio broadcast. Every day he expected to
hear news of the Allied invasion. But May passed
without any change in the war, except that the nightly
bombing raids on Germany were becoming heavier.
During one of the last nights in May, a thousand planes
passed overhead on their way to Cologne. And the Ruhr
was under constant bombardment. They heard a song
on Radio Orange that ended with the refrain:

> But in the early light of dawn
> They saw the factory was gone,
> Except for Jerry's favorite john.

June, too, passed without an invasion. By then Fritz
had lost heart. Despondent, he even passed along
William's latest joke, which was far from optimistic.

"Have you heard the story of the woman who had
such a beautiful dream?" he asked. "One morning she
woke her husband and said to him, 'Honey, you know
what I dreamt? I dreamt peace had finally come, and

then I saw an airplane landing in Rotterdam's airport and an old, grey-haired lady got out. And do you know who it was?'

'Yes,' said her husband, 'Princess Beatrix!' "

Princess Beatrix was the oldest daughter of crown princess Juliana, who had gone into exile in Canada. In his disillusionment, Fritz sometimes felt that the pessimistic husband in the joke was right and that this dreary war would go on forever.

But during the last week of June, the English did make an appearance—and much closer than Fritz had expected. Because he was such a sound sleeper, however, Fritz almost missed the event entirely.

That day the bombers had started coming before nightfall, one formation after another. The eerie ebb and flow of droning planes sounded like the distant roar of hungry beasts prowling through the night. With the first rumble of engines, Hanneke had fled into her parents' bedroom, where she slept peacefully in the safety of Mother's arms. The others were so accustomed to the sound they no longer heard it. Uncle Gerrit even said that he had trouble sleeping when it was quiet.

But this particular summer night John couldn't sleep because it was so muggy. He lay in bed with his eyes wide open, listening to the throb of the engines. Then he got up and sat on the windowsill to watch the distant searchlights probing the dark sky. Bright flashes lit up the horizon, sometimes three or four in quick succession and then a muffled detonation would sound from afar as if a thunderstorm were approaching. They were the evidences of the bombings of Emden and Bremen, not far across the German border.

According to the Nazi-censored papers, these bombs were doing very little damage. German fighters were supposedly keeping the English planes away from the cities so that they were forced to drop their bombs out in the countryside, where all they ever killed were a few cows. But the news broadcasts from England and the workers who were home on furlough from Germany told quite a different story. Hamburg, Bremen, Cologne, Berlin, and many other German cities had been hard hit and were being completely leveled!

John could just imagine what they must look like! He had been in Rotterdam after it had been bombed on that horrible day in May, 1940. Rotterdam and Warsaw were being cruelly avenged. Every flash of lightning meant more buildings destroyed and more bodies torn apart. Women and children were being buried under the rubble. Were they also guilty of what had happened to Rotterdam? Was their crazy baker right? With almost every loaf of bread that he delivered, he declared with an oath that the Germans were a disease upon the face of the earth, and that they should all be drowned in the Zuiderzee!

Look at that flash! They must have dropped a whole string of bombs that time. You could see the fire splashing upwards against the sky! As John stared into the night, which was dark once more, and listened to the howl of planes passing overhead, he imagined the horror that was raining down on the German cities. He shivered and noticed that the night was getting chilly.

He sought out his bed again, and with a shudder he

pulled the blankets up around him. These were terrible times! It seemed as though the world had gone mad. Why did all this have to happen? Wasn't the earth big enough for everyone to live side by side in peace? Wasn't there anyone who could put an end to all this suffering? He lay there, feeling absolutely powerless to help.

Only God could do it. You could pray and ask Him to please hurry, of course, and John was sure that thousands of people must be doing so every day. But why didn't God put a stop to it? He lay there, turning over and over in his mind without finding an answer. But he was certain of one thing! It was the blind hatred of people like their baker that caused wars. Suddenly he understood why Mother had said that the man's bread had lost its flavor. Father had laughed, but soon another baker was delivering bread to the house; a timid fellow who didn't dare say a word about the war. That wasn't right either, but it was better than the snarling vindictiveness of the other man.

Finally John dozed off. It seemed as if he had slept for only a minute when he was again leaping out of bed and dashing to the window. A deafening racket rocked the house! It sounded as though English and German fighters were battling directly overhead. The rattle of machine guns and the crack of canons almost shook the windows out of their frames. Fiery streaks went shooting across the sky and briefly lit up John's entire room.

He heard a door open and close and footsteps hurry down the stairs. Quickly pulling on some clothes, he too went running down the stairs and outside.

Dawn wasn't far off. You could sense it, rather than see it. The wonderful coolness of the morning air mingled with the scent of grass and flowers. John took a deep breath. The shooting had stopped, but the droning continued unaffected. The bombers were on their way back home, flying fast to get out of hostile territory before daylight. The short summer nights increased the hazards of an already perilous flight.

"Is that you, John?" a voice asked.

"Ye...."

"No, Uncle Everett, it's me," another voice said at the same time. It was William. Uncle Gerrit, too, had left his room over the garage, for suddenly he appeared at John's side.

"Ho-hum!" yawned Uncle Gerrit. "That rooster was a little early this morning. But someone must have wrung his neck, because I don't hear a thing anymore."

Then they heard a new noise in the sky overhead. A shrill whine pierced the dull rumble of the bombers and became a plaintive moan. It must have been a fighter plane making a sharp turn just above the house. Suddenly machine guns began chattering.

They pressed themselves against the wall of the house and, standing side by side, watched the dogfight overhead. Then a loud bang shattered the air, and a bright flame shot across the sky! It disappeared for a moment. But when it reappeared, it mushroomed until it lit up the whole yard. They could see the outlines of a large aircraft angling earthward, wrapped in a ragged shroud of flames.

Shouting at each other to watch out, they ducked down. The fireball was plummeting straight for the house! Wailing like a fury, it passed over the roof and came crashing down several hundred meters beyond with a tremendous thunderclap!

Then it was over. The sky was dark again, and the steady drone of the returning bombers continued as though nothing had happened. But not far away, out in a wheatfield, a huge fire began to glow. And a blackbird sitting high in the pine tree next to the house began chirping happily as though he had mistaken the light for the rising sun.

As if by a prearranged signal, they all began running into the orchard in the direction of the burning plane. They passed close by the farm of Harry Hoeks, where they heard loud voices. So Hoeks and his boy would soon be there too. Father was the first to come to his senses.

"What are we doing?" he shouted to the others. "There's no helping whoever's in there!"

They stopped in Hoeks' pasture. The dark shadows of the cows were milling between them and the fire. But what was that? Among the shadows of the cows there was another shape. The flickering light from the burning plane made the shadows shift and leap across the meadow. It was the form of a man. Slowly it came toward them, haloed in flames. "Good morning!" it shouted, in English. "Are you friends?"

They stood as if petrified, staring at the man.

"Are you friends?" he repeated. "I need civilian clothes. Can you hide me?"

Father was the first to regain his voice. "Yes! Yes, we can!" he answered. And suddenly William whooped, went running toward the man and, grabbing hold of him, pumped his hand. Then the others also crowded around and shook his hand. He was one of the fliers from the downed airplane. His parachute lay at the other end of the pasture. The cows had collected around it and were sniffing at it curiously.

Uncle Gerrit came up just then on his stiff old legs. "Did you find one of those umbrella jumpers?" he shouted. "How do you do, English! You can call me Uncle Gerrit. Shoot, you can call me Aunt Emily!"

William, who spoke fluent English, translated for them. He told them that the flier's name was Jim and that he was the tail gunner on the plane. He had been the third man to bail out. The pilot, badly wounded, had been unable to jump.

"Poor Bud," the Englishman said, looking toward the fire, which was blazing up higher now, casting a red glow over their faces.

"He needs civilian clothes," said William. "What say, Uncle Everett? We're not going to let the Krauts get him, are we?"

William seemed to have forgotten all about the trouble his previous contact with English fliers had caused him. And Father seemed to have forgotten it too.

"Come on, hurry!" said Father. "Get that parachute from the other side of the fence, William, and bring it to Uncle Gerrit. Then we'll take this man back to the house with us. You and John go and look for the other fliers. Make sure nobody sees you, and don't leave anything behind to show they've been here."

A few minutes later, he disappeared into the darkness with the English flier, heading back across the fields. Uncle Gerrit followed him, his arms filled with silk and rope. William and John jogged farther into the pasture. It was starting to get lighter now. They heard voices approaching from all sides as people hurried toward the fire. Figures were moving around the burning airplane.

The flames were beginning to subside, however, and by the time they reached the plane, it was little more than a pile of smoking ashes from which protruded a tangled skeleton of red-hot angle iron and steel tubing. They couldn't get very close because of the blistering heat. Across the fields came a car, bumping over the furrows.

"Krauts!" said someone.

"Let's get out of here," whispered William. "I don't have my papers with me."

They ducked behind a windbreak. From there John took one last look at the wreck. He was deeply troubled at the thought that here in a pasture close to his home lay the ashes of a young Englishman, who only a few hours before had been alive, laughing with his friends. Again he was overwhelmed by the conviction that a world where such horrors occurred had to be raving mad.

John and William quickly circled in the direction of the house. Looking back, they saw people being chased away from the plane wreck, and could hear the Germans barking orders all the way where they were standing. The Nazis always seemed to be shouting.

At the house everything was quiet. Only Uncle Gerrit was outside. He was digging beside the manure pile. That old man could surely work! But what was he doing?

When they came up beside him, they saw the parachute—no, two parachutes—half hidden under some loose straw. Two?

"The other umbrella-man landed in Hoeks' yard," explained Uncle Gerrit, wiping his forehead. "George is his name. John, run into the woods and make sure Wallinga isn't sniffing around. Hurry, get the lead out! Willy boy, get yourself a manure fork and give me a hand."

After looking around, Uncle Gerrit picked up the parachutes and dropped them into the hole he had dug.

"What are you doing!" exclaimed William. "You're not going to throw those away, are you? That's beautiful silk! You could use it in all sorts of ways!"

"Sure, but we can use *you* in all sorts of ways too," said Uncle Gerrit. "And if the Germans saw you with some of this stuff, we wouldn't get the chance. Now stop jawing and carry some of those rocks over here. Hurry! Didn't they teach you how to work in that there doctor's school?"

They dropped the rocks on the parachutes to pack them down in the hole. Then Uncle Gerrit pushed the dirt back in. Last of all, he and William moved the manure pile squarely on top of the hole.

From his vantage point in the woods, John had a good view of the Wallinga place. Everything seemed to be business as usual over there. The hired hand was just driving the wagon out to the pasture to do the milking. Wallinga crossed the yard carrying a pail and disappeared into the barn. So he hadn't even gone to look at the fire! Maybe he was afraid of the crowd. Recently he had found out what people really thought of him.

About two weeks ago, as he was passing through town one dark night, a pair of unknown assailants had ambushed him and thrashed him with willow branches. The talk was that one of the Hoving boys had been the instigator. The Hovings were a bunch of firebrands and refused to kowtow to anybody. The police had failed to catch the attackers. Maybe that beating had wised up the old Nazi sympathizer.

As John emerged from the woods, he ran into Father, who was heading toward the camper with a bushel basket filled with supplies.

"What in the world are you doing strolling around in the woods?" Father asked, irritated. "You ought to be lending a hand. Run up to the house and ask Mother for some salve for burns and some bandages. And tell her to make some coffee!"

Father was obviously overwrought, so John didn't bother to defend himself. He just hurried toward the house. Uncle Gerrit and William were still busy at the manure pile. William was still wearing his pajama top.

"He ought to change," thought John. "If anybody drops in, they'll get suspicious." But it was four-thirty in the morning, an unlikely hour for anybody to be dropping in. Mother was in the kitchen making coffee. She too was upset, John sensed, even though she acted calm. She handed him the first-aid kit and warned him to be quiet. She didn't want the younger children to wake up. Fritz, too, slept through all the hubbub.

When John neared the camper, he smelled the pungent smoke of an English cigarette. Inside, the kerosene lamp had been lit, and Jim was changing into an old suit of Father's. It seemed to fit him quite well. The other flier, George, sat on William's bed, smoking. He clutched one hand in the other. It was red and swollen. The left side of his face was also badly scraped. But he managed a friendly smile as John entered the camper, and digging in his pockets, he came up with a pack of cigarettes.

John would have loved to take one, but it was too dangerous. When he told Father that he had smelled the smoke outside, everybody was immediately ordered to douse their cigarettes. John wanted to stop and chat a little with the English fliers—they looked like nice guys, not much older than William—but Father sent him on another errand, fetching blankets.

"Here, take this bushel basket and put the blankets in there," he said. "Keep an eye out for William, and tell him to come here when he's finished with what he's doing!"

By the time the children woke up, everything was shipshape. The men in the camper had been served sandwiches and coffee and were presumably fast asleep. William was on guard to help them escape in case the Germans came to search the farm and their hiding place was threatened.

At breakfast Father sat in his usual place by the table. He was a little quieter than usual, but outwardly just as calm and easy-going. Not until then did Fritz and Margy, their young housekeeper, hear about the plane that had crashed in the pasture. Fritz wanted to go right out and take a look, but there wasn't any time—he had to leave for school.

John, Tricia, and Fritz biked to school together. Tricia had been in on everything, so she gave John a meaningful look when they saw German soldiers scouring the countryside. They couldn't say anything because of Fritz, but they could see the worry in one another's eyes. Those soldiers were searching for the crew of the English plane.

What would happen if they found the two men in the camper? John knew the answer very well. The lives of the two fliers weren't in any danger. They would only be sent to a P.O.W. camp. But Father and William and probably Uncle Gerrit would be arrested, and after a quick trial, they'd all be shot. This had happened in other towns across the country. Maybe they would also arrest Mother, and they might also put the torch to the house. The Nazis were very hard on anyone who helped parachutists. They were well aware that an underground railway existed to help downed fliers get back to England via Belgium, France, and Spain, so that they could get back into the fight.

Wasn't it foolhardy, John asked himself, to risk the future of the entire family just to keep a couple of strangers out of German hands? Was this part of the general madness that had seized the whole world? He was still mulling it over as he sat in his desk at school. But he knew what was mainly bothering him: fear. Fear was making him ask these absurd questions.

No, this wasn't the work of madmen. Mother and Father weren't doing this out of hatred, but out of love and obedience. Mother had said: "Hide the outcasts; don't betray the fugitive." And he remembered that Father had been nervous and scared that morning. Mother too. But they had both done what they considered to be their duty, without hesitating. Well, wasn't it his duty to be there with them to help, instead of lounging here in a comfortable desk learning irregular French verbs? If something happened, he wanted to be home!

When the French lesson was over, he couldn't stand the suspense any longer. He reported sick to the principal and asked for permission to go home.

"Yes, by all means," said the principal. "You look awful! Do you need someone to go along with you?"

Naturally, John said that he could manage, and he hurried out. In the hall he saw Tricia with some girls from her class. They were just changing rooms. When he told her that he had reported sick and was going home, she winked and said, "I thought of doing it myself. Be careful!"

On the outskirts of town he was stopped for an I.D. check, and then again when he was almost home—the first time by a policeman and someone in civilian clothes, and the second time by German soldiers. They were checking everyone's identification. But as he cycled up their street, the house was still standing peacefully in the midday sun, and the soldiers were no longer searching the fields. Parked in the driveway, however, was a strange car. When John got closer, he saw a medical emblem on the window and realized who it was. Father emerged from the woods with the doctor.

"What are you doing home?" he asked John.

"I wasn't feeling well, so I figured I'd better come home."

Father looked him in the eye and laughed. "Don't worry, son," he said throwing an arm around John's shoulders. "Everything's under control. Well, doctor, if they ask you, here's your patient."

"Not necessary," he said. "I stand on the secrecy of the doctor-patient relationship. I never tell the Nazis where I've been. Medical ethics, you know. Just last week two Germans came to my office. Had I treated a fellow for a bullet wound? I knew what it was all about.

"A fellow escaped when he was being transferred. Jumped out of a speeding car. They shot at him and were sure they hit him. If I'd said, 'No, sir. I didn't treat him,' they would have narrowed it down to one of the other doctors. So I said, 'Sir, you may not ask such questions of a doctor. The privacy of the doctor-patient relationship is protected by law.' You should have seen their faces!"

Laughing, he climbed into his car. "Call me, if you need me," he said. "Just say your youngest has a bellyache; then I'll know. Cheerio!" And he backed down the driveway.

"Listen, John," said Father. "If you've got nothing else to do and you're not too sick,"—he gave John an affectionate dig in the ribs—"you might take your bike and pedal around the neighborhood and keep your ears open. See if you can pick up any scuttlebutt on the whereabouts of the third flier. Okay? But be careful! And come right back here and tell me if you hear anything peculiar."

CHAPTER SIX

It wasn't John, however, who picked up the trail of the third flier, but Uncle Gerrit. He was helping Harry Hoeks put up his hay, as he often did during the busy season. It was about eleven o'clock in the morning, and Uncle Gerrit was sitting on top of half a load of hay in a field across the road, when number three came squirming out of the weeds along a small canal along the field. "Hello!" he hollered, standing up. He was a short fellow with a little mustache and a big grin.

Uncle Gerrit quickly checked in all directions to see whether the coast was clear. "Come on, Hoeks," he said. "There's our last flier-flopper. We might as well make our round-up complete. Drive this wagon over there, and let's get him tucked under the hay before the little rooster crows the whole German army down on us."

"Yes, but . . . but . . . ," stuttered Hoeks, who didn't

feel cut out to be a hero.

"But . . . but nothing!" said Uncle Gerrit. "You want him to fall into the hands of the Krauts? They took your best horse and three of your best cows, and now they're after your son!"

Hoeks shut his mouth and whipped up his horse. It was true! He had an account to settle with the Germans. He drove the wagon close to the edge of the ditch.

"Up here!" said Uncle Gerrit, signaling to the flier. "Look at him, will you! Doesn't he have a lovely mustache? That should be great camouflage; it blends right in with the hay. Give him a hand, Hoeks. Come on, English! You look like you'd be great fun on a hayride."

Uncle Gerrit pulled the flier on top of the wagon and pushed him into the hole he had dug in the center of the load. Hoeks drove the wagon back to the middle of the field. "Head down!" said Uncle Gerrit, pushing the flier's head down, and he quickly piled hay on top of the man. Then they went on stacking the shocks of hay onto the wagon to get a full load before heading home.

"Keep those shocks coming, Hoeks. The sooner we get this wagon loaded, the better!"

Suddenly Uncle Gerrit remembered something and went diving back into the middle of the hay. "Your umbrella! Where did you leave your umbrella?" At first the flier didn't know what the old man meant. But then he surfaced and pointed to the trees, babbling something Uncle Gerrit didn't understand. Uncle Gerrit shook his head, "No English! No verstand!"

Then the Englishman held his nose and pointed to the

woods, "Jerries . . . Krauts . . . bang-bang!"

"Blast!" said Uncle Gerrit and pushed the flier's head down again. So the Germans were after him! That complicated things.

"Hurry, Hoeks! More hay!" Then he made a mad dive at the flier. The idiot was about to light a cigarette with hay up to his eyebrows!

Uncle Gerrit snatched it away. But what should he do with the cigarette? He couldn't very well toss it out into the field; the Germans might see it. Quickly, he stuffed it into his mouth and chewed on it as if it were chewing tobacco.

The Englishman shook with laughter. He seemed ready to enjoy himself no matter what happened. Uncle Gerrit covered him up with hay so that he couldn't move a finger; only his head was at the surface so he could breathe. Finally the wagon was loaded, and Uncle Gerrit and Mr. Hoeks were just finished tying down the load when they heard voices. At the far end of the field three German soldiers emerged from the woods. They jumped the small canal and cut across the field toward the wagon. One of them was carrying a parachute.

"Shhh! Krauts!" Uncle Gerrit whispered to the Englishman. "Keep your trap shut!" And then he dropped another shock of hay right on the flier's head.

"You see any enemy fliers?" yelled one of the Germans in German.

But Hoeks didn't understand any German; he stared at the soldiers uncomprehendingly. Uncle Gerrit, however, had spent some time in Germany in his youth, and he remembered quite a few phrases. Chewing on the

cigarette, he looked down on the German soldiers and shouted, "Sieg heil! Guten Morgen! Was wollen Sie? Fliers? Ja, jawohl, gentlemen! Last night. Rat-tat-tat-tat! Boom, boom! Crash! Kaput! Burnt . . . gebrennt. Over there!"

Yes, the soldiers knew about the airplanes. But the fliers, the men—had they seen any of *them*? One of them must have come down in the trees over there. They showed the two men the parachute. They had found it snagged in a tree! Uncle Gerrit had to listen to quite a story, for the soldiers had noticed that he understood German. But he was impatient to get going; he wanted to get his load home. And he had to get rid of his mouthful of tobacco or he would gag. He spat down alongside the wagon, and one of the soldiers jumped to avoid being hit. He cleared his throat again, and the man took another step back.

Uncle Gerrit mopped the sweat from his face with his old cap.

"We're working men around here," he said. "We don't go hiking around in the woods. All we see is hay, hay, hay—all the livelong day. Over there! Da! Englander poof . . . verbrennt! Last night!"

The soldiers shook their heads and turned away. "Heil Hitler! Auf wiedersehen!" they said. But Uncle Gerrit was already telling Hoeks to get the wagon rolling. The flier was clawing at the hay to clear it off his head, but Uncle Gerrit rapped his knuckles with the handle of his pitchfork. In spite of his confident appearance, the old man felt weak with nervousness. It had been a close call! Nevertheless, he was a little disappointed with himself.

"Try it again, you blimey limey, and I'll use the other end on you," he growled. The flier laughed, and Uncle Gerrit heaped another armful of hay on his head. He resisted the temptation to look back at the soldiers until they had reached the road. When he dared to take a quick look, the soldiers were just disappearing into the woods.

They crossed the road and drove into Hoeks' large barn. The wagon stopped by the hayloft, and Uncle Gerrit helped the flier dig himself out. Fifteen minutes later, he was walking rapidly across the fields beside Uncle Gerrit, dressed in a blue work shirt and a pair of overalls with the pantlegs rolled up to fit him. They cut through the orchard and made a beeline for the camper. There, flier number three was received with such noisy jubilation that William almost had to get angry before they quieted down. The new arrival was named Art.

After being fortified with coffee and sandwiches, he lay down on Jim's bed to rest. There were two more bunks in the camper that folded down from the wall above the other beds, but more blankets had to be fetched. The camper was becoming a tight squeeze.

Father ordered William to see to it that no one spoke above a whisper. The area still wasn't safe. The Englishmen badly needed an overseer, for they soon forgot themselves. They were so carefree that they would have gone for a stroll in the woods if William hadn't been there to stop them.

All day long, small groups of German soldiers searched the area; and in the early afternoon, five of them crossed the street into the orchard. They were headed straight for the woods containing the camper. John was the first to see them. He felt as though he were suddenly impaled on a bayonet of fear, but he controlled himself and quickly warned his parents.

Mother grabbed little Hans out of his playpen and took five-year-old Trudy by the hand and walked out through the front door. She looked calm, but John had never seen her so pale. Father grabbed a small suitcase that was already packed, and he and John headed in the direction of the Hoeks' farm. At the edge of the orchard, they stopped behind a clump of trees.

"If something happens," said Father in a firm, quiet voice, "you catch up to Mother and walk with her into town. Don't rush. In town you catch a bus and take her to the Kramers. Stay there until you hear from me. Don't worry about me! I've got contacts. Pick up Fritz and Tricia at school so they don't go home. You got that? Do you have any money?"

With his eyes fixed on the woods, he pulled his wallet from his pocket and handed John several bills. His hand was steady, but his jaws were clenched. John felt himself drawing strength from his father. His fear ebbed away, and he was suddenly filled with confidence and determination. He knew he could do his part.

The minutes dragged by until, suddenly, the Germans came crashing out of the woods. They stopped a moment to get their bearings and then cut across the fields in the direction of the plane wreck.

"Thank God!" breathed Father, and he closed his eyes for a moment. "John, you tell Mother. No, don't run, just walk. Calmly!"

A short time later they were back in the house, together again. Mother began making tea. Father went to check on the men in the camper and returned to say that everything was fine. The German soldiers had passed within a few yards of the camper. The fugitives had heard their voices and remained absolutely still. The hideout had passed a severe test.

The danger was far from over, however. The Germans continued to patrol the area and made spot checks along the roads. They also began to search homes near the crash site. But they skipped the De Boer house. They probably thought it was too small to house fugitives, so they focused on the large farm homes in the area, which were filled with likely nooks and crannies.

On the third day, a Saturday, John and Fritz had an unexpected encounter. They ran into Schram, the N.S.M. plainclothesman whom they had come to know in Scheveningen at the beginning of the war. He had been transferred to this district and had caused the family two days of intense anxiety when Father had been imprisoned as a result of Schram's treachery.

This particular afternoon, the two brothers had biked to the Hoving farm to pick up sacks of oats for turkey-feed. It was against the law to sell oats, because the distribution of all cattle feed was supposed to be controlled by the government. But out in the country, no one paid any attention to the law, especially on Saturday, for then there were very few checks along the roads. The inspectors who patrolled to uncover black market activities had to have their days off too.

The Hovings were just sitting down for coffee when the boys arrived, so they were invited to join them. As they sat in the kitchen drinking coffee, through the window they saw a tall, skinny man in a seedy-looking overcoat come walking onto the yard, pushing his bicycle. He turned up the path leading to the side door of the house.

"Wonder what that weirdo's doing here?" Hoving asked no one in particular.

John leaped up to get a better look, and then he was sure! That rabbit face and those jutting ears—it couldn't be anyone else! "On your toes! That guy's dangerous, Hoving. He's a N.S.M. cop!"

Fritz cried in recognition, "Why, he's the guy that . . . ," and then he clamped his mouth shut. He wasn't sure how much he should say, even here.

But Hoving had heard enough. He hurried the diver, who was sitting with them drinking coffee, out of the room. "Here, take your cup with you!" They heard footsteps in the summer kitchen, and then a soft, timid knock on the door.

"We'd better answer the door," whispered Mrs. Hoving. But her husband motioned her to stay where she was. The big, powerful farmer didn't seem to know the meaning of the word *fear*. He detested those of his fellow countrymen who had joined the N.S.M. and regarded them as traitors. This afternoon he was in a mood to avenge himself a little. He straightened up in his chair and fixed his eyes on the door.

"Come in!" he bellowed.

Hat in hand, Schram came sidling into the room. He

nodded so deeply that he was almost bowing. He told them his name was Mulder—John and Fritz looked at each other—and that he was from the city, where it was hard to get food. He asked the farmer whether he could spare a couple of eggs, because his wife was sick, and the doctor said she should have eggs.

Then he was silent, and he scanned the group sitting around the table. His eyes briefly touched on John, who didn't look much like a farmhand in his blue blazer, but he didn't seem to recognize him. John had changed quite a bit during the last two years.

"Are you finished?" asked the farmer.

"Yes, sir," said Schram. "You see, I'm just a clerk, so I don't make much . . . ."

"Then you should join the N.S.M.," Hoving said with a straight face. "They'll see to it that you get plenty of everything. We're never short of anything, right wife?"

Now Schram didn't know what to think. Was he among comrades here? He hadn't been invited to sit down, but he gingerly perched himself on the edge of one of the kitchen chairs.

"But I can't give you any eggs," the farmer continued unsympathetically. "We National Socialists must avoid becoming part of all this black marketeering and smuggling, don't you think? I turn in all my eggs to the distribution office as I'm required to do. What you should do is go to the authorities and request a special ration card for your sick wife. Right?"

Schram nodded miserably.

"And you should know that, my man!" snapped the farmer, as if he were angry. "I should hardly have to remind a pencil-pusher like you of the law!"

"I-I didn't know you were a member of the party," stammered Schram.

"But so are you," said Hoving. "Otherwise you wouldn't call it 'the party.' Anything else I can do for you?"

Schram sighed, eyeing the coffee pot. "I guess that's all . . . ," he said. "But haven't there been a lot of planes passing over lately? I heard that one of them crashed somewhere around here. You think all those fliers burnt up with the plane?"

"I haven't the faintest idea," replied Hoving. "I wasn't there." John could tell he was trying to figure out what Schram was after. But John knew, and he felt increasing disgust for the man. He should have guessed it. The rabbit was out scouting for the Germans.

"I've heard that a couple of them landed safely and that they're being helped by farmers around here," probed Schram. "Have you heard anything like that?"

"Listen," Hoving said quietly, as if in confidence. "I guess I'd better tell you."

"Yes?" said Schram, leaning forward.

"That you're a dimwitted numbskull!" the farmer exploded. "If I knew anything, I'd have told the Germans, of course. We go by the book here, see! But you—you're something else! You're a disgrace to the party. I don't trust you as far as I can throw you. What are you anyway? An English spy? A black market dealer?"

"No, no!" protested Schram. "You've got me all wrong."

"What do you think, Bert?" Hoving asked his son.

"I don't trust him either. I think we should tie him up in the barn and call the police," said Bert.

"I'm sorry you . . . I assure you . . . . Honestly, I'm a loyal member of the party."

"You take us for fools?" shouted Hoving, rising. "You think farmers are a soft touch, eh? If you don't get out right this instant, I'll kick you clear back to England, you lousy spy! Bert, turn the dog loose. That'll hurry him up."

But Schram was already running toward the road with his bicycle. He kept looking back for the dog, which never came. The farmer roared with laughter, and the others also chuckled at the sight of the fleeing collaborator. For a moment John almost felt sorry for the man, but then he and Fritz told of their past run-in with the man and how that had led to Father's imprisonment.

When Hoving heard the story, he said, "Too bad, boys! If I'd known that, I'd have taken Bert's suggestion and tied him up in the barn."

"Yeah," said Bert. "I'd have trussed him up good and tight so he couldn't breathe and then gone looking for a cop out in the pasture."

But all the farmers weren't as bold as Hoving, nor did they all have the advantage of being forewarned. As John and Fritz were pedaling home an hour later, they saw Schram emerging from another farmhouse, chatting with the farmer's wife as she handed him some eggs from a pail. He seemed to have had some success there. John hoped that all he had gotten from the woman were eggs. It was a good thing that no one in the area knew about their guests!

As soon as they got home, Fritz and John told Father what had happened at the Hovings, and John saw a glint enter Father's eyes that he had never seen there before. All Father said, however, was, "So, he's still as dangerous as ever, is he? Now he's working as a German spy! We'll have to keep an eye on him. I'd better drop in on Hoeks a minute. Schram might stop for eggs there too."

Shortly after Father had left, the telephone rang. John answered it.

"Hello, is this Everett De Boer?" asked a voice.

"No, this is John De Boer, his son."

"O John, it's you. Well, you can pass on the message to your dad. This is Vander May. Tell your dad that I'll pick up the puppies at eight tonight."

"Okay," answered John. "I'll tell him right away."

"Whatever you do, don't forget!"

"No, sir, I won't. Goodbye!"

John didn't wait for Father to return but immediately headed for the Hoeks' farm to pass on the message. They didn't have any puppies, but John could guess what the message meant. He had met Mr. Vander May before, so the latter knew that John was in on his father's secret work.

Vander May's real name was Jansen, and he was the chief of police in a city not far from there. Most people took him for a Nazi collaborator and a member of the N.S.M. and that was all right with him. His reputation had won him the confidence of the S.D., the

German security police, and he was a frequent visitor at S.D. headquarters. Actually, he was one of the most important resistance leaders in the area. John suspected that he had helped Father obtain William's new papers.

At exactly eight o'clock, a police car drove into the yard with Mr. Jansen at the wheel. Hansie, Trudy, and Hanneke were in bed, and Fritz had been sent into town on an errand, so the coast was clear. John called the fliers while Father talked to Jansen. William accompanied his English companions to the car. Art had exchanged his farm clothes for a suit. Now they all looked like city dwellers and should arouse no suspicion in town.

Quickly, they piled into the car. But first they wanted to say good-bye to Mother, who had fed them so well. John had to run into the house to get her. Jim kissed her hand, and Art hugged her. All three of them invited Mother and Father, William and John to visit them in England after the war was over.

Jansen started the car—just as Fritz came pedaling into view.

"Goodbye!" shouted the fliers. "Be seeing you! God bless you!"

Fritz was just in time to catch the parting words, and his mouth dropped wide open. He watched the car drive away. Then he threw down his bike in the driveway and burst into tears.

Father put an arm around his shoulders, but Fritz shook it off.

"Get away!" he sobbed. "I know who that was! But you don't tell me nothin'! You don't trust me!"

"Honest, Fritz," pleaded Father, "I trust you as much as I trust myself, but it's not good to let more people in on things than is absolutely necessary. What you don't know, you can't be held responsible for. If John hadn't just happened to be there, I wouldn't have told him either. But if I need you for something, Fritz, no matter what, I'll let you know, and then I know I can count on you. And listen . . . ."

He took Fritz aside and whispered something in his ear. Suddenly Fritz flung his arms around Father's neck and kissed him. Then, embarrassed about what he had done, he threw a few jabs at Father, prancing around like a boxer. Father's delighted laughter rang through the quiet evening. John could tell that a tremendous load had been lifted from his shoulders.

That night, when the younger children were asleep, the rest of the family sat together in the living room. Father dug a pack of cigarettes out of his pocket and handed one to everybody, including Fritz. They were in a Dutch package, but they were English cigarettes, considerably better than the usual wartime fare. He had been given them by the English fliers, but to be on the safe side, he had destroyed the English wrapper.

While they all sat blowing smoke at the ceiling, William related everything that the fliers had told him about what was going on in England, about the tremendous arsenal that was being built up in America, about the preparations that were being made for a gigantic invasion, and about the second front that would be launched later in the year, now that England, America, and Russia had become allies.

Their hearts filled with hope, and the room was awash with dreams. Was it possible? Could the war still end this year? That night they felt as if they had already won a small victory.

Mother and Tricia were in the kitchen doing the dishes and harmonizing on a hymn that summed up all their longings and hopes. Mother was singing again! It suddenly struck John that he hadn't heard her sing for quite some time.

"Quiet! Shh!" said William, who had the sharpest ears in the family.

"Brrroommm, Brrroomm . . . ."

It was the first wave of English bombers—the first wave of a flood that inundated the night.

CHAPTER SEVEN

After that night, it seemed as if peace would never again return to the De Boer household. Everybody for miles around seemed to know that this was where they could come for help when they were in danger. Maybe the sheltered location of the house was an attraction too, for it stood on a quiet road well away from town and could be reached from several directions by forest-lined dirt roads.

For the past several months, in the days following one of Father's turkey deliveries, several people would stop by the De Boer place. Among them were a farmer's son, a teacher, two girls, and a retired gentleman. They would report to Uncle Gerrit in the garage, sometimes stopping to talk with Father, and when they left, they had bundles of *Free Holland* stuffed in their bicycle bags or under their clothes. These papers would be distributed in their respective towns. Sometimes, Mr.

Vander May dropped by and sometimes a nameless but familiar fellow from *Free Holland* headquarters. This had all become part of the De Boer household routine, and they were all used to these visits.

One evening the mayor of a neighboring village unexpectedly appeared on their doorstep asking if he could stay overnight. He barely knew Father, having met him only once at a conference, but his pastor had told him that he would be safe at the De Boers. The Germans had ordered him to supply them with a list of all the Jews living in his village. He had refused. Now he was afraid that they would come and arrest him in the middle of the night, as was their practice.

So, of course, he was invited in. Mother could never turn away a fugitive, not even a mayor, she said with a smile. So another diver joined the household. First, he came only to sleep, but after a few days he no longer dared to return to his home. Uncle Gerrit gave him his best coat, and the children called him Uncle Steward for no one was supposed to know who he was.

The farm could use an extra hand in the orchard, because it was in the middle of the fruit season. Father, too, worked out in the orchard all day; after all, according to his I.D. and the records in the town hall, his official occupation was now fruit grower. This change in occupation had saved him from being called up to work in Germany. But the mayor was no fruit picker. He ate more than he picked, said Uncle Gerrit. And after he had picked a couple of basketsful, he complained about bursitis in his shoulder. Uncle Gerrit wasn't heartbroken when he lost his helper a week later.

Uncle Steward had received word that he had been deposed as mayor and that the Germans were looking for him to arrest him. Father falsified the mayor's papers—a job he had learned to do himself. Uncle Gerrit suggested that Father change the mayor's occupation to fruit inspector, for then the Germans would get no more apples from Holland because the mayor would eat them all. Father made him an inspector for the C.C.S., the Crisis Control Service instead, and with this new identity he set out for relatives in another part of the country.

No sooner was this guest gone, than new trouble appeared at the door. This time it was two of John's older schoolmates, Ron Mulder and Art Van Dyk. They had graduated a few weeks ago and now were looking for a place to dive. They came in looking much as William had when he first arrived: spooked and jumpy, only partly successful at concealing their fear. With them, they brought the shocking news that Carl Van Bergen had been arrested. Carl was the friend who had showed John his cartoons and awakened him to the work of the resistance.

A week ago he had left on a sketching trip to the coast. His plan was to map out the defenses that were being constructed along the entire coast. Carl had found a way to smuggle this information to the English, said the two friends. But that afternoon someone had called from Schoorl, a town on the coast, to say that Carl was critically ill. This could only mean that he had been taken prisoner. So it was no longer safe for them to stay at home, because they had been working very closely with him. The German interrogators might force Carl to reveal their names or some other incriminating information.

The De Boers couldn't very well refuse to help a couple of John's friends who had gotten into trouble for helping the resistance. Therefore, they too were invited in and put up in the camper with William. But after they were over their first scare, they proved to be dangerous guests. Restless in the confines of the camper, they went gallivanting about the neighborhood at night, devising all kinds of mischief. They found the sign that Father had swiped, "We Don't Serve Jews," and hung it on Wallinga's front door.

The same night, they went into town and set fire to a string of railroad cars loaded with hay destined for Germany. Fortunately, the police concluded the fire had been started by sparks from a passing locomotive and the investigation went no further. When Father went to tell them the good news, he found them taking potshots at rabbits in the woods around the camper.

Furious, Father confiscated their guns and told them if they didn't shape up, they could leave that same day! The following day they helped pick apples and entertained little Trudy, who had taken a shine to the two boys. The next day, however, she was walking around the yard singing a little song that the boys had taught her:

> Hitler stares, Hitler glares
> Through his basement windows;
> "Oh, where's Berlin?" the Fuehrer blares.

He wipes his eyes and blows his nose.
"Is it safe to come upstairs?
Everytime that siren blows
And English bombers fill the air,
Dust and plaster spoil my clothes,
And I need a change of underwear."

Things quieted down considerably when the two boys went back home a week later. The reason they could go home, however, was tragic. A messenger had arrived from Schoorl to tell the Van Bergen family that Carl had not been arrested, but that he had been shot while photographing the coastal defenses. However, he had been carrying a forged I.D., and the Germans had no idea who he really was. His body had been disposed of by the Germans, so his parents would never know where he was buried.

The devastating news affected John for days. Once he awoke in the middle of the night to see the specter of Carl Van Bergen standing by his bed, smiling. Carl had always been a jovial, out-going fellow. John could still see him mounting his bike with a flying leap and greeting everyone with an enthusiastic wave of his arm. He had always been so full of life that you couldn't stay somber when he was around.

Now he was buried somewhere with a German bullet in his body. It seemed impossible, but it was true. In a fraction of a second, a small piece of lead had snuffed out all that life and talent. He might have gone on to great things if he hadn't become involved with the underground. Why had he done it? He could have stayed in the safety of his room sketching and painting. Was the work that he had been involved in worth such a tremendous sacrifice?

How old was he? Twenty, at most. He was about two years ahead of John and had graduated just one year ago. John remembered the day that Carl had taken him up to his room and showed him the cartoon. Their friendship had started when John had expressed his eagerness to help distribute the cartoons. When they had shaken hands, it had been a kind of pledge—to each other, to their country, and to the cause of freedom. But now one of them was dead.

What about himself? He was still alive—but for how long? He didn't want to die. He wanted to live and go to college and become an architect, like his father, or maybe a writer. And he wanted to travel and see the world. And maybe someday he would build a house somewhere, as his father had done, and raise a family.

But tonight that all seemed like an impossible dream. A very different future seemed to be cut out for him. All he could see ahead of him was the war. Should he refuse to have anything more to do with it? Refuse when Father asked him to deliver illegal newspapers or ration cards for divers? And should he try to talk his parents into sending William away and turning away all fugitives in the future? How could he do that? He would despise himself, and then life wouldn't be worthwhile anymore either.

Father was right. Once he had said, "It's a funny thing about resistance work: you don't want to do it, you don't dare to do it, but when it comes right down to it, you can't *not* do it. It's as if God were telling you to do it. And if we know we're acting in obedience to God, we no longer have to weigh and calculate the odds and live in fear. Then our lives are in His hands."

This finally brought some peace to John's mind. In fact, suddenly he felt himself to be very much in the will of God. It seemed as if he could see Carl in the darkness, looking just like he had when they had sealed their pledge with a handshake. John slipped out of bed, checked the blackout curtain to see that it was closed properly, and then switched on the light. He sat down at his desk and began to write. It was as if he were getting one last chance to talk to his friend. The words came spontaneously, with their own rhythm and rhyme.

To Carl Van Bergen

Once you showed me the way, my friend,
when your laughter tore the sacred veil
of tyranny. Now I tremble for my end,
fearing our lives were bound to no avail.

There are words I wish we'd spoken:
thoughts we shared but left unsaid.
Despite death, our bond remains unbroken,
and our pledge is far from dead;

for not our own cause did we choose,
nor do we stand or fall in our own frailty.
We march with Him and cannot lose,
for all His soldiers are already free.

John read it through once more, hesitating at "the sacred veil of tyranny." Didn't that sound a little too romantic? But he let it stand, thinking of the goddess of the French Revolution. Carl hadn't died for that kind of liberty. She was one of the goddesses that he would have punctured with his cartoonist's pen. When he read the poem over in the light of morning, he let it remain as it was. He copied it over, signed it "John," and addressed the envelope to Carl's parents, without adding a return address. Maybe it would give them some comfort as they grieved a death they couldn't even acknowledge publicly.

From that day on, John was a changed man. He was both more serious and more carefree; he had once again discovered direction in his life.

The summer vacation had begun, but no one in the De Boer family wanted to go anywhere. Where would they find a place more peaceful than out here in the country? Besides, travel was difficult, and again rumors persisted that an invasion was imminent. Their two aunts from Rotterdam and Uncle Herman and Aunt Haddie visited them for a couple of weeks. And despite all the stories that they told of repression and persecution and food shortages, they had a good time together. When they left, moreover, they looked considerably better than when they had arrived.

Then the summer vacation was over, and for several weeks nothing special happened. But one evening the farmhouse had another visitor—this time, a woman. A bus stopped not far from the house and dropped off a young lady. John was just taking a breath of fresh air out front, and he recognized her immediately. It was Rita, the young nurse from Rotterdam.

He sprinted down to the road, walking the last few steps. And then he was face to face with her. She still had the same refreshing smile and the same teasing twinkle that she had had two years ago.

"Well, John, here I am!" she said, as if it had been only two days since that time. John felt the blood rushing to his face. He'd thought of her often in those two years; he had even written several poems to her which he had never sent. But she didn't seem to notice his confusion. She put out her hand, shook his, and at the same time thrust her suitcase at him.

"What a beautiful place to live," she said, admiring the house and its setting. "How peaceful and pastoral. Boy, you seem to have grown John! At least, you've sure put on weight in the shoulders. Your face has even changed.

"John, do you think I could stay overnight? Unless you've joined the N.S.M.; then I won't darken your doorstep."

John laughed and said, "If you don't come in, I'll report you for activity hostile to the state—to the state of my mind."

As he walked her to the house, Tricia was standing by the window watching them approach. "Look, Mom, I'll bet it's that little nurse that he met in Rotterdam two years ago. I can tell by the way he's looking at her. Do you think he invited her here without telling us?"

When Tricia turned out to be right, Rita got an enthusiastic welcome from Mother and Tricia. They were just setting the table, so Rita was immediately invited to join them for supper. When Father came in a few minutes later and was introduced to Rita, John was dumbfounded to hear Father thanking her for her help in getting the medical excuse for William. Without John's knowledge, Father had contacted the loyal little nurse to help establish William's identity as a teacher on medical furlough.

"There's your patient," he told her, pointing at William.

"I still feel terrible," said William, clutching his head. "I could use some intensive care by a pretty nurse. Otherwise, I might suffer a horrible relapse."

"I have better things to do than to look after spoiled medical students," she told him. "I'm here for someone else."

"Does she mean me?" John thought to himself. "Has she had me on her mind all this time?"

But after supper John found out the real reason for the visit. In the studio, Rita told them that she was here for a Jewish girlfriend, who had roomed with her in nursing school. The girl had been working in the same hospital with Rita, although she should have been fired over a year ago, for the Germans had banned all Jewish doctors and nurses from the hospitals. But they had obtained an Aryan I.D. card for her, and she had kept working. Her features, however, were quite Jewish, and she avoided going into town, except to visit her aging parents.

Her parents had grown more and more reclusive as a result of the harsh measures that the Nazis were taking against Jews. They were no longer allowed in the theaters and parks; nor were they permitted to travel on the streetcars or buses. Their money and property had to be registered, and they had to turn in their radios, bicycles, and cars. Finally, they were forced to move to specially designated ghettos, separated from the rest of their countrymen. Socializing with non-Jews was also forbidden; in fact, Jews were allowed on the streets only at certain times to do their shopping, and then they had to wear huge yellow stars.

But things were going to get worse, said Rita. She and Esther—that was her friend's name—had tried to persuade her parents to go into hiding. But the old couple had stubbornly shaken their heads. No, they didn't want to; they didn't dare. For then if they should be discovered, they would certainly be shipped out—first to a camp in Holland, and from there to Germany—then they would never see their family again.

They could better go on obeying the Germans, they said, for then maybe they would be left alone. The Germans couldn't very well arrest all the Jews in the entire country, all the women and children, could they? Even the Germans didn't blame the women and children for anything, did they? No, Esther's parents couldn't believe it! The Germans would leave them alone as long as they did what they were told. Besides, maybe the war would be over soon.

But the terrible day had come! The Germans were starting to round up Jews by the thousands. Trainload after trainload were being shipped to Germany. They were ordered to turn themselves in, and most of them went. What else could they do? Rita had been told of one little old grandmother who had gone to turn herself in and had innocently asked the German officer, "Is this the headquarters of the Jewish persecution?" And she had been struck down on the spot.

Rita's eyes darkened and her face grew pale with anger as she told her story. She and Esther and others had managed to rescue quite a few people, and place them in non-Jewish homes. Especially children. It took much searching to find willing families, for most people were far too afraid of the Nazis to help the Jews. When they had been placed, then came the task of getting ration cards and false I.D.'s for their divers.

Food was hard to get in the cities, even for those with ration cards. Sometimes, after they had been at a certain address for a while, Jewish children suddenly had to be moved because their foster parents had been frightened by something. Frequently, there *was* real danger, but sometimes the danger came from the foster parents themselves, who demanded payment for their help.

Soon this work kept them going night and day. Esther had been the most courageous, the hardest worker of them all, but now she had been picked up. She had been betrayed by one of her patients, and had been arrested after work one night as she was leaving the hospital and heading for home. For many days nothing had been heard from her.

But three days ago, Rita had received a letter from her; it had been smuggled out of a transit camp at Westerbork not far away. It was a letter of farewell, for she had no hope of getting out alive. She had been put in a special barracks for hard cases, and she expected to be shipped off to Poland very soon. Her next stop, she had written would be a death camp. But, cried Rita, that couldn't be allowed to happen. They couldn't just let her go off to her death! She had saved so many others. Rita wept silently.

"What did you have in mind?" asked Father. "What can we possibly do for her when she's in that camp?"

"I don't know," Rita said, wiping her eyes. "I thought maybe *you* could think of something. You're the only person I know in this part of the country."

Father didn't answer. He was lost in thought. Suddenly, John asked him, "Don't you think there might be some way, Father? You remember that soldier you lent some clothes to in Scheveningen? Remember when we visited him—how close his farm was to the camp at Westerbork?"

John would have done anything to help after seeing the pain in Rita's eyes. How he would love to be the one to change that pain to joy!

"Yes," said Father, "that was the camp. And if you remember, the place was surrounded by ten-foot barbed-wire fences, many watchtowers, and S.S. guards. What could we do against that?" Father lapsed into silence once again. Then a couple of minutes later, he jumped up. "I'm going to give Vander May a call." Father dialed a number and waited. Suddenly they heard footsteps outside in the gravel, and the figure of a man darkened the window.

"Look there!" cried Rita, frightened. "Who's that?"

"Vander May!" shouted Father. "Well, what do you

know. Isn't that a coincidence! Come on in! You just saved me a phone call."

"That's a good sign," said Rita, smiling again. And she seemed to be right.

When the policeman had heard the whole story, he said to her, "You're right. We've got to try to get that girl out of that camp. We'll see what we can do. I'm sure I can contact her.

"A number of Dutchmen have been forced into guard duty at the camp, and I know one of them. He hates the whole business passionately, and if he gets the chance to help one of the prisoners, I'm sure he'll take it—even if it means that he might have to go into hiding himself. Maybe we can give him his chance.

"We've got some other things going for us, too. Several large transports of Jews arrived there in the last two weeks, so it's chaos inside the camp. They've put in three tiers of bunks in the barracks, and there are still hundreds of people sleeping on the floors. Tomorrow I'll drop in on this guard—let's call him Nick—and ask him to try to find Esther."

"Make sure he gives her my love," Rita urged.

"Fine! That will do her good. If Nick proposes an escape plan to her, she won't be too frightened to carry it out, will she?"

"Esther? Esther isn't afraid of anything!"

"Good! Then we need someone to take over outside the camp. That would be a good job for these two young swashbucklers. Do you know the area, John?"

"Not very well," replied John. "I've been there only once with Dad."

"You'll have to study it, then. I have some maps and a layout of the camp at home. You come home with me tonight, and I'll let you have them. You'll have to memorize them so that you don't have to take them along. If you were picked up carrying something like that, it'd be curtains!

"Tomorrow, you two go to Westerbork and ride around the camp on your bikes so that you'll know the area first hand. Pay special attention to the southwest side of the camp. That looks to me like the best approach. As a matter of fact, just last week we smuggled someone out from that side. You'll have to have a reason to be nosing around out in the fields around the camp. Do you know anything about botany or zoology? No? Well, it's probably too late in the fall anyway."

"If Tricia and Rita went along, we could be two young couples on a little outing," suggested William.

"That's not a bad idea," said Mr. Vander May. "Do you have enough bicycles? Otherwise, I can lend you my wife's for Rita. What's the matter, Everett?"

"I'd rather we kept the young people out of this," said Father. "Why don't I go and scout the camp myself?"

"Do I hear the voice of an anxious father?" Vander May asked, laughing. "Don't you worry, Everett. It's a good plan. You'd draw attention if you started nosing around there. These kids are sharp, and maybe they'll see things that we would miss. Let's give them a chance to show what they can do."

John already found himself trembling with eagerness to get going.

"Chin up, Rita!" said Vander May as he turned toward the door with John. "We won't fail our comrades in Rotterdam. There's hope! As long as there are loyal people like you, there's hope."

CHAPTER EIGHT

The weather was in their favor. Groups of men and women were harvesting potatoes out in the fields as Rita and Tricia, William and John cycled toward Westerbork and the camp. It was a perfect day for a bike trip, and when they reached Hooghallen, not far from the camp, all four of them were in an eager, confident mood.

That mood didn't last long, however. As they stood in the little village taking a breather, a train pulled into the station and began disgorging hundreds of Jewish men, women, and children. They were quickly herded into long rows by the waiting S.S. to be marched to the nearby camp.

As the two couples pedaled on, they ran into another column of people headed for the camp. They stopped to watch this tragic procession, but were ordered to move on by one of the guards. So they rode on until they got to a farm where a group of people were standing on the lawn, watching. There they rode up the driveway and stopped.

The Jews that filed by were all from the city. There they went, side by side, the bank director and the laborer from the produce market, the wife of the used-clothing dealer and the family of the importer of the latest Parisian styles. Venerable old gentlemen and strong young men, mothers with children in their arms and an old woman who had to be supported on both sides—all of them wearing big stars with the word "Jew" embroidered in the middle. Everyone carried suitcases and packages and bundles of blankets. They plodded along, their faces expressionless. The shuffle of feet and the soft murmur of voices was periodically shattered by the hoarse shout of an S.S. officer: "Schnell, schnell! Hurry up there! Close ranks!"

"Oh, John, it's awful!" whispered Tricia grabbing his arm.

John didn't answer. He didn't trust his voice. Something throbbed deep in his throat. The stream of people seemed to go on forever. How many people had the Germans packed onto that train? Occasionally there was a break, but soon there would be a new column following the one that had passed. From the farmyard, the young people could follow the progress of the human herd along the winding country road. Between the sunny fields filled with ripening crops, a long, dark snake slowly made its way forward. Finally, at the tail end of the procession came a horse and wagon stacked high with boxes and suitcases and clothes. On top of the load, between two lolling and grinning S.S. guards, sat a doddering old man whose head flopped from side to side with every jolt of the wagon.

But the procession wasn't over! Chained behind the wagon came a handsome Jewish boy of about fifteen. His hands were bound behind him, and he fought every step of the way, yelling and struggling hopelessly. He reminded John of the story of Joseph: how he had been tied behind a camel after being sold into slavery by his brothers. Of all those hundreds of people, he was the only one to protest and give vent to his indignation and pain. But the wagon dragged him on, and the two S.S. guards only laughed. And no one dared to help the boy.

"Like sheep to the slaughter," said a man standing behind John. The farmer suddenly began shouting and cursing at the Nazis on the wagon. Wailing in fear, his wife ran toward him to try to silence him, but he seemed to have gone berserk! Still screaming curses at the Germans, he was dragged off into the barn by a couple of other farmhands.

"That doesn't do much good," someone said. And when John looked toward the voice, he found himself staring into the face of Schram, dressed in the same seedy overcoat that he had been wearing that day at the Hovings. John quickly turned, taking William by the arm and pulling him toward their bikes. From there, he pointed Schram out to William.

"I bet he's prowling around for the Germans to spy on the people who live around the camp," whispered John.

William stared at Schram with such undisguised venom that John wished he hadn't said anything.

"Let's go," said John, "or else he might recognize me."

William said he had to get a better look at "this insect," and he went off, slowly circling around the man to study him from all sides.

"We've got to know our enemies, and know them well," said William when he returned. John looked at him. There was something frightening in his voice.

They got back on their bikes in silence, not knowing what to say to each other, and they pedaled away faster than before. Their goal was near, and the purpose of their trip had suddenly become very clear and vivid—even if it was only to rescue a single person out of that endless procession.

There were quite a few people standing along the road. Were they merely spectators who had heard about the arrival of a trainload of Jews and who had come to satisfy their curiosity? Or were there also friends and relatives of the deported Jews among them? A young farm boy who met them on his bicycle shouted at them, "Watch out! Check ahead!" But they went on. Their I.D.'s were in order. William had passed through such checks before with his forged I.D., and he didn't worry about it anymore.

Two men in civilian clothes stopped them. One of them spoke with a German accent.

"Zo, you are from Rotterdam?" he asked William, studying his I.D.

"That's what the card says," replied William.

"You haff some special interest in de Chews?" He fixed two sharp eyes on William, but William didn't blink or waver.

"The Jews? What could I have to do with the Jews?" he shrugged. "Though, you've got to admit it isn't a pretty sight—all those people herded along like cattle."

"Where do you liff in Rotterdam?"

"That's also on the card," said William. "Number 28, Zwart Street."

"Yess, I see. And how are you coming from your house to de station?"

William hadn't figured on such a question, and he hesitated a moment. He couldn't very well have memorized the whole city map of Rotterdam! Memorizing the map of Westerbork had been hard enough. But William quickly recovered.

"Oh!" he said, laughing. "Now I get it! You don't believe that I'm from Rotterdam! You want to know how to get from Zwart Street to the railroad station? That's not so easy. Which station do you mean?"

"Vell, de one vhat is closest, of course," said the German.

"So you want Central," said William. "Okay, let's see. You follow Zwart Street to Wallenburger Road, turn at the Christ Our Savior Catholic Church, take number nine to the Queen's Boulevard and then you're there. It's on your left, across from . . . ."

"All right," said the man. "Go on!" And he handed William's I.D. back to him.

"It's a good thing he's got a good memory," John thought, as he hopped back on his bike.

But as soon as they were out of earshot of the inspectors, Rita began giggling uncontrollably. "Boy, you've got nerve!" she sputtered at William. "Wallenburger Road! That's way at the other end of the city! You made it all up."

"Of course," said William. "Just as long as I convinced that guy. I just said a few names that happened to come to mind. At first he scared the liver out of me! But when it sank in that he had asked for *the* station, I realized that he didn't know Rotterdam any better than I do."

This incident put them all in a better mood. By the time they had biked along the canal a way and found a pretty hollow where they could eat their picnic lunch, they could almost persuade themselves that they were really out on a holiday outing. William and Rita were constantly teasing each other. They were a good match. John felt himself growing a little jealous. Compared to William, with his easy charm and banter, he felt himself to be awkward and dry. And Rita must feel the same way about him, he told himself.

He checked his watch. "Hey, listen," he said. "By now those people must have arrived at the camp. This would be a good time to nose around a bit. I bet everyone will be busy with the new arrivals."

"Great idea," seconded Rita. "Come on. Let's go. Should we take the bikes or should we walk the rest of the way?"

After talking it over, they left the bikes in a clump of bushes and followed a trail that led in the direction of the camp. They oriented themselves by the tall chimney that rose from the camp laundry. Soon they came to a large yellow sign in German, forbidding them to go far-

ther. They paid no attention to it, except from that point
on they tried to always keep bushes and trees between
themselves and the camp. The area was dotted with
blackberry bushes loaded with ripe blackberries, so they
began picking them by the handful. Soon their hands
and lips were blue with blackberry juice. They couldn't
have asked for a better justification for being there.

The trail came to a swampy area and then divided.

"We should follow both trails to see where they
lead," suggested William. "Let's split up: two of us one
way, and two the other. Look for a trail that leads close
to the camp. If we come here in the dark, we don't want
to end up in those swamps."

"Good idea," agreed John. "Which of the girls is
going with you?"

William snorted. "You think I'm blind, lover boy?
Come on, Tricia, stick close to your leader!"

Keeping under cover of the underbrush as much as
possible, John and Rita drew closer and closer to the
camp. They saw the tall watch towers constructed from
rough-hewn pines and the armed guards at the top.

Suddenly they smelled a strange, putrid smell. It
reminded them of dirty, mildewed clothes and lysol. It
was the smell of the overcrowded camp, where thousands of people had been crammed together into a few
barracks.

John grabbed Rita's hand and pulled her into some
bushes.

"This is far enough," he whispered. "We can see
enough from here." He pulled the branches apart to get
a better look at the camp. "I hope William has better

luck," he added quietly. "We could follow the trail this far, but then we'd have to follow the barbed wire, and the ground is dotted with holes and swamps over . . . ."

A sudden sound—was it a cough?—made John whirl around, but he whirled right into Rita's embrace. "Kiss me!" she whispered. "Come on, kiss me!"

John was so dumbfounded, he didn't react, so Rita threw herself at him and kissed him full on the mouth.

"Hey you! What's going on here?" a loud voice demanded.

Rita's arms tightened about his neck, and she kissed him again. Then she twisted away and, giggling, said, "Yipes! You scared us! What's the matter?"

Behind them stood a big German soldier, his rifle aimed straight at them. He tried to scowl, but he had a hard time suppressing a grin.

"You're not supposed to be around here. Can't you read?"

Rita looked around as if searching for a sign.

"No, back there!" the soldier pointed. "Didn't you see the big yellow sign?"

"We didn't see any sign. We were just out picking blackberries," said John.

"Didn't see it, eh? No, I don't suppose so. That's love! Eyes only for each other," he said with a smirk. "But if you want to smooch, you'd better find someplace else. You can't do it here. This is a camp—a camp for Jews."

"Pew!" said Rita, pulling a face. "So that's what smells around here—all those stinking Jews. Come on, John. Let's go!"

She leaped up, stepping past the German. She put a friendly hand on his sleeve as she squeezed by, pulling John with her. The guard didn't object.

"Congratulations," he said to John. "You've got yourself a pretty girl!" And although the compliment came from a German, it still thrilled John.

"Thank you," he said politely.

He put his arm around Rita and strolled back down the trail with her. He felt himself trembling, but it wasn't because of the German guard. He still hadn't recovered from Rita's assault. That had been much more disturbing than the guard.

"Rita," he began, "I know we haven't seen each other for a long time, and . . . well, I like you a lot, and . . . well, I wanted you to know."

"I do know," she said, stopping. "And I like you too, John." Then she threw her arms around his neck and kissed him again. This time he kissed back. Rita turned around and threw a kiss at the German guard, who motioned them to keep moving.

"If somebody else sees you, they might take a shot at you!" he shouted.

Walking arm in arm, they quickly made their way back to the bikes, where William and Tricia were already waiting. William was all excited as he told them that he and Tricia had found a perfect trail: it passed within fifty yards of the camp.

"Good!" said John. "That's the one we'll have to take, because the fork that we took runs into some rough terrain."

That's all they said about their little adventure; they

had agreed to keep the rest a secret. But Tricia gave John a searching look and then grinned mysteriously. She knew her brother too well for him to be able to hide anything that important from her.

But she didn't ask any questions, for which John was thankful. On their way back, they dropped in on Mr. Peeks, the soldier who had a small farm across the canal not far from the camp. John found him out in the field harvesting potatoes and partially filled him in on the plan. Without hesitating a moment, the farmer volunteered his help. He showed them how to get across his land to the trail that William and Tricia had scouted.

It was already getting dark when the foursome got back home. Mr. Vander May had already stopped by, said Father—with good news! The guard had agreed to do everything in his power to help Esther. After he had made a plan how to get her outside the camp, he would contact them as soon as he could. It was important that they move as quickly as possible, he stressed, because the camp was getting overcrowded. A shipment of Jews would be sent to Germany any day, and those in the special barracks in which Esther was housed were always the first to go. This last bit of information made Rita sick with worry. How horrible it would be if, just when everything was set, they would be too late!

But Vander May was back again the next afternoon with word that the wheels had already started turning. They had to make their attempt that very night, for a train was due to leave the camp for Auschwitz tomorrow or the next day. Nick, the guard, had spoken to Esther. They had gotten another break: because so many people in the camp were falling sick, Esther had been released from the special barracks to help care for them. This made things easier.

Nick would see to it that she arrived at the barbed-wire fence on the southeast side of the camp between watch towers VI and VII some time between one and two o'clock. He would help her under the wire, and he would also try to arrange to have friends in the two nearest watchtowers who would be willing to doze off for a while. William and John would have to get as close to the fence as possible, because Nick was staying inside. He didn't want to go into hiding until it was absolutely necessary. The password was "Rita," and the answer would be "Esther."

"Have you got it all?" asked Vander May. They nodded. "Then I want both of you to repeat everything back to me."

Each of them recited the plan without a single slip. They planned to take Esther along the route that Peeks had showed them and hide her in his house until morning. In the morning, Vander May would pick her up in the police car. But where would she go from there?

"She's welcome to stay here—in the camper," offered Father. "William could join Uncle Gerrit over the garage."

Rita, however, thought Esther should return to Rotterdam as quickly as possible, for in Rotterdam she had many friends, all of whom would be more than willing to hide her. Moreover, maybe she would be able to return to her nursing duties after a while.

"But she doesn't have any identification," Father

reminded Rita.

No, that was right! Her I.D. would have been confiscated.

"Do you have a photo of her?" Vander May asked Rita.

Yes, Rita had a snapshot, one that could easily serve as an I.D. photograph.

"Then we're set," decided Vander May. "Say, Tricia, you think you could manage to lose your I.D.? Nothing would help us more right now than if we just happened to come upon a stray I.D. card."

"I've always been good at losing things," said Tricia with a laugh.

"Good! Let's have a look at it. See? It's perfect. We remove Tricia's picture, replace it with Esther's, then touch up the seal and we're all set. What do you think, Everett? Can you get that done tonight? Thanks, Tricia. Tomorrow you'd better go to the police station and tell them you've lost your I.D. They'll give you temporary papers that will get you by for the time being, and then you'll get a new card in due time."

"You're making liars of all my children," Father said to Mr. Vander May, grinning. "After the war I'll have to start all over again teaching them the difference between truth and falsehood."

"Not a chance!" said Vander May. "Tricia knows very well that she's telling a lie in order to serve the truth, right Tricia?"

"Not a lie, a military stratagem," said William.

"Lie or military stratagem, I don't think I'll lose much sleep over it if it helps get Esther out of that death camp! I'm only too glad to be able to help."

Father immediately took Tricia's card and Esther's picture into the studio, while Vander May once more reviewed the layout of the camp with William and John. He assumed that, because the boys had done the scouting, they were also to do the actual rescue work. Father once again raised objections, especially when Vander May talked about arming both boys. But in the end, he reconciled himself to the idea, although his eyes were filled with anxiety. Father produced one revolver and Vander May lent them his. He took his police revolver from its holster and explained how it worked.

"Be careful," he pleaded. "If you're caught with this thing, I'll have to go into hiding myself! It's stamped with a serial number registered under my name. On the other hand, don't hesitate to use it if necessary. Give the handguns to Rita to hide under her clothes until you get to the Peeks' farm. Make sure you take along your raincoats. Just look at that sky. Unless I miss my guess, we'll get some rain tonight."

They were ready to leave at four o'clock. Tricia was disappointed that she wasn't going along, but she no longer had an I.D. John strapped Rita's suitcase to the back of his bike. It contained a full change of clothes for Esther, which had been donated by Tricia. The farewells were emotional. Mother struggled to keep back the tears.

"Please be careful, John," she begged. "William, you take good care of him!"

"Don't worry," said William. "John's quite able to take care of himself. He's not a boy anymore. Isn't that right, Rita?" he added, grinning at her.

Fritz came running out of the orchard to shake hands with them. The solemn way he did this showed he too understood the danger his brother and William were going to face. Uncle Gerrit was raking leaves out of the driveway, and he too had some parting words.

"Well, Rita," he said, "it really pains me to see you go. I was just beginning to gather the courage to ask you to marry me. I'm young and strong, only seventy-two years old, not overly homely, and I've got a great job here. Dare I hope, or is my suit hopeless?"

Rita was quick on the uptake.

"Oh, my dear sir!" she said, putting on the look of a coy maiden. "Would you give me a few days to consider? I'll give you my answer by letter."

Uncle Gerrit chucked her under the chin, and went back to his raking. Before they passed out of sight, John looked back one more time and saw the old man standing at the foot of the driveway staring after them.

Before they were halfway to Westerbork, it began to rain, and it didn't let up the rest of the way. As a result, dusk came a half-hour earlier than usual and by the time they were cycling up the forest road leading to the Peeks' farmhouse, it was completely dark. While they shed their dripping raincoats, they caught the smell of frying bacon coming from the kitchen. Soon the three young people were sitting around a purring stove, each with a cup of coffee and a bacon sandwich, while the steam rose from their damp clothes.

Mrs. Peeks, a hefty, motherly woman, insisted that they take off their shoes and socks, which had become drenched on the long bicycle trip. As they tried to relax, waiting until it was time to go, Mrs. Peeks dressed her children for bed in the heat by the stove. When they were tucked in for the night, she poured more coffee and sat down with them as Mr. Peeks described how he fooled the German farm inspectors and managed to slaughter three pigs a year for his family instead of only one as decreed by the occupation government. It would have been a nice, cosy evening, except for the unbelievably slow "tick-tock" of the old cuckoo clock.

At eleven o'clock, William and John could restrain themselves no longer. They put their shoes and socks back on and went outside to take a look around. The rain was still coming down steadily, and it was so dark that the earth seemed to have swallowed them up. They hurried back into the summer kitchen connected to the house. There Rita joined them to give them their revolvers, which were still warm with the heat from her body. They checked the guns by the light of a gas lantern standing on the table, hurriedly concealing them when Mrs. Peeks entered the room. Yawning, she suggested to Rita that she try to get a little sleep while the boys were gone. But Rita thanked her and told her that she wouldn't be able to sleep anyway. She would just as soon sit in the big easy chair and wait.

When they went back inside, Mrs. Peeks had already gone to bed. Finally, it was nearing the time for them to go. John and William put on their raincoats, and Peeks pulled on a pair of boots. Rita kissed both boys, acting casual as if they were only going to town on an errand. But John was conscious of her eyes following him into the darkness as he and William were led across the yard by the farmer. It filled him with a sense of the meaning of life and a determination not to fail. No matter what happened, Rita wasn't going to be ashamed of him!

Mr. Peeks accompanied them to his property line. By then they had become used to the darkness and could pick their way between the black shapes of bushes and trees.

"I'll wait for you here, starting at one o'clock," the farmer whispered. "If I hear something, I'll whistle like this," and he imitated the shrill wail of the lapwing. "If you respond, then all is safe, and I'll lead you up to the house. This is the trail. Feel the sand underfoot? Well, good luck, boys. Better not talk once you get out in the open, for sounds carry a long way across this grassland."

The rain drummed on their raincoats and hissed in the grass as they silently sought their way along the saturated trail. William led the way and appeared to have memorized the route pretty well. Occasionally stumbling over ruts and hollows, he moved along with surprising sureness. Then suddenly he stopped. Shhh! He had heard something.

There it was again! The noise was close to the trail. John moved and his raincoat flapped alarmingly in the night. A frantic rustling exploded past them as a startled rabbit went splash-splashing away through the wet meadow. Soon John again smelled the stench of lysol. At the same time, William turned left off the trail and stalked forward very slowly with John right behind him. They stopped. Ahead of them the wet uprights of a watch-tower glistened in the faint glow of light that spilled from one of the barracks. That had to be tower VI.

Slowly they retreated a little, counted out about fifty yards to the right, and again turned to creep toward the camp until they were within a few feet of the barbed wire. Then they sat on their haunches in the high grass. After a while their legs got cramped, so they lay down on the wet ground and surrendered to the pouring rain.

The glow of light from the barracks had disappeared. They were surrounded by darkness and the soothing sound of the rain. Was this the place where the girl would soon appear? To John it seemed impossible that they could have found the right spot in this black expanse. Doubt it or not, he had to rely on William, who had led them here without hesitation. He could hear William breathing next to him, and he was flooded with a sense of comradeship. He wanted to reach out and touch William, but instead he groped for his revolver. He had thrust it into the outside pocket of his raincoat so that it would be easy to reach. It was a strange sensation to feel the heft of the revolver in his hand. He found himself clenching his teeth. Would he be able to use it if necessary? He tried to imagine a German soldier discovering them in the grass and raising the alarm. Yes, he would shoot, all right. Before the other guy got the chance.

What time was it? John pulled up his left sleeve and peered at the face of his watch. The glowing hands were close together, so it had to be almost one o'clock. She should be here any time!

A noise! Someone was coming. Voices sounded near

tower VI, and now they could see a flashlight beam dar-
ting about. A man with a flashlight was walking toward
them along the barbed wire. He must be on the inside,
for the fenceposts were between them and the light.
Someone else was walking behind the man. A hand suddenly pressed John's head down. With his head against
the wet ground John peered between the weeds,
tightening his grip on his revolver. They were opposite
John and William now, their boots splashing heavily
through the puddles. If the guard shone the light
through the fence . . . .

"Stinking weather!" a voice complained. "I'm sure
glad to be down from there. Is there any coffee left?"

They had passed, and John noticed that he hadn't
even been scared. He felt pleased with himself. The men
stopped to talk at tower VII, and then everything was
quiet again. Up in the tower a match flared momen-
tarily. The guard must have lit a cigarette. So this had
been the changing of the guard! Were the men who were
now up in the towers the friends of Nick who had been
tipped off and who knew that they were here? John felt
the suspense beginning to build.

Suddenly a loud voice echoed in the camp. A man
shouted something unintelligible—it sounded like German. Was it a guard sounding the alarm? But nothing
further happened. The leaves on a nearby shrub began
rustling; the rain was letting up a bit, but a breeze had
sprung up. Time passed very slowly. One-thirty. Had
something gone wrong inside? What if she still weren't
here at two? They would have to wait, of course. Until
dawn if necessary. John shivered. Something was

tickling his throat and he jerked his coat over his mouth to cover his cough. The noise still drew a poke in the ribs from William. Was something stirring, about ten yards to the right? The barbed wire twanged and hummed.

"Come on!" whispered William. He rose into a crouch and moved toward the sound. John followed him.

"Rita!" said a man's voice, rather loudly.

"Esther, Esther!" they answered in unison.

They jumped up. A dark figure rose from the ground just outside the wire. Esther! John's throat was taut with emotion. There she was—Rita's friend, picked up on a busy street in Rotterdam and marked for death, and now, here in the darkness of this northern grassland, she was being returned to the living.

"Have a good trip," a voice whispered. "Now make tracks!"

William had the girl by the hand and pulled her away from the barbed wire into the dark meadow. As John followed them, he noticed that he was carrying the revolver in his hand. He looked back. Everything was quiet. He might as well put it back into his pocket.

He felt the sandy trail underfoot.

"Take over," said William. "I'll go ahead and find the best way back."

John took the girl by the arm. She seemed poorly clad for a wet, chilly night—all she wore was a dress. Or was it an overall? The stench of the camp clung to her clothes. What was that? She was making strange muffled sounds. She was crying.

"I can't believe it!" she sobbed quietly. "I can't

believe it!''

"Shhh!" warned William. "We haven't made it yet!"

"Rita's waiting up for us," John whispered to divert her mind.

He felt like crying himself, he was so thankful. But he was too busy trying to keep up with the dark shadow that bobbed ahead of them.

Kee-weet! Kee-weet!

The call of the lapwing! For a moment John wondered if perhaps it were the real thing. Then the voice of Mr. Peeks came out of the darkness: "Congratulations! Follow me." And he led them on toward the farmhouse.

The climax of the escape came when the two girls met each other in the doorway of the kitchen and rushed into each other's arms. Mrs. Peeks came hurrying into the kitchen too, dressed only in her nightgown. "Is it her? Is it her? Oh, my, look at her! She's drenched to the skin. Let me stoke up the stove!"

Now the two boys turned to see what they had helped to rescue: a frail-looking little thing dressed in ugly blue overalls with hair cropped close to the skull.

"Good grief, Esther!" cried Rita, breaking into tears. "What have they done to your hair? Those animals! Oh, your beautiful hair!" But then she got hold of herself. "No matter. It will grow back. Let's get you out of those wet overalls. Where's my suitcase? You boys make yourselves scarce for a while. Here are your cigarettes. I'll call you when it's all clear."

The three outcast males retreated into the summer kitchen where they sat smoking by the light of a gas lantern. Mr. Peeks lit up his pipe. Suddenly William whooped and wrestled John to the floor, where they tumbled around like schoolboys until a revolver went clattering to the floor. Then Rita appeared in the doorway to tell them that it was safe to come back into the house.

The women were already drinking coffee, Mrs. Peeks still in her nightgown. Esther was almost unrecognizable now that she was dressed in Tricia's clothes. Despite her cropped-off hair, she was quite pretty, especially because of her beautiful dark eyes. They sat around the table, and while Mrs. Peeks made sandwiches, Esther recounted her side of the escape. A German guard loitering around the hospital barracks had almost spoiled their plans. Nick, the guard helping Esther, had been forced to wait until the man moved along. As she described life in the camp, however, Esther began to grow more and more agitated, until Rita forbade her to go on.

Rita made her friend sit in Mr. Peeks' easy chair and put a kitchen chair under her feet. Mrs. Peeks brought several pillows and fixed a place for Rita too on the other side of the stove. The two older people then said goodnight and went to bed. After turning down the lamp, William put his head down on the table and closed his eyes. John took the only remaining easy chair, quietly sliding it close to Rita's.

A stillness settled on the house, accentuated by the peaceful tick-tock of the clock.

A hand touched John's, and a sleepy voice whispered, "Oh, John, I'm so happy . . . so happy."

It was a night that John would never forget. Morning

came all too quickly, and Vander May was tapping out the letter *V* on the window. Fifteen minutes later, he was gone again. With him went the two girls and the revolver. The girls were to be put on a train to Rotterdam, carrying a suitcase loaded with cheese and lunch meats.

Two days later the De Boers received a postcard from Rotterdam addressed to the De Boer family. It was signed: "Rita and Tricia, With Deepest Thanks." So they had made it home safely. The next day a card arrived for Uncle Gerrit. On it was the picture of a seductive gal with a come-hither look, inscribed with the words, "Forever yours!" Grinning triumphantly, the old man showed the card to John.

CHAPTER NINE

After this, the De Boers found themselves in the thick of the struggle. The persecution of the Jews had been going on for several months. Raids and huge transports were constantly being organized all over the country. The De Boers had heard the Nazi program denounced in church, and had read gruesome accounts in the underground press, but until now all the suffering had left them largely untouched. By helping to rescue Esther, however, they had become personally involved. Less than a month later they were hiding four Jewish divers.

Rita had brought them a nine-year-old girl from Rotterdam. As soon as Mother caught sight of those frightened dark eyes and the pale little face, the matter was settled. The child's beautiful black hair had been changed to blond with a generous application of peroxide, and now she went by the name of Marie De Boer. She was passed off as a niece from the coastal town of Scheveningen who had been forced from her home by the evacuation.

Marie was treated like one of the family and went to school with Hanneke. The evacuation story sounded believable because thousands of families had been forced to move out of the coastal areas where the Germans were busy constructing fortifications against the anticipated invasion. Many other evacuees had already arrived in the district.

Even Hanneke believed the story, and so did Trudy, of course. They were just a little surprised, however, to discover that Uncle Herman and Aunt Haddie had a little girl, because they had never met her before. It was amazing to see how well Marie played the role that Mother had taught her. She almost seemed to have forgotten that her name was Sarah Goldsmit and that she was one of three daughters of a Rotterdam banker. When people asked her, she calmly replied that her home was in Scheveningen near the dunes, at 85 Dune Street and that her father was a teacher, and no, she didn't have any brothers and sisters.

"And where are your mother and father now, Marie?"

"Oh," little Marie would say, "Father got a job teaching in Amsterdam, but he couldn't find a place to live, so he and mother are staying in a boarding house. But there wasn't enough room for the three of us, and the doctor said I should get lots of fresh air, because I was in the hospital for a long time. And that's why I'm staying with Uncle Everett and Aunt Grace."

She would recite everything with her big innocent eyes

fixed right on the questioner. Yes, she thought it was wonderful here, and she wasn't very homesick for her Mom and Dad. Anyway, she would see them at Christmas.

Sometimes she was teased that if she kept eating the way she was, her parents wouldn't recognize her when she got home, because she was turning into a chubby little farm girl, but she never laughed. She never laughed at anything. She no longer seemed able to. At home, everyone in the family tried by turns to get a little laugh out of her, but with no success. Even when Uncle Gerrit put all his talents to work, he succeeded only in getting a dutiful little smile from Marie.

Two weeks after Marie had moved in, Mr. Liebstadt arrived with his wife and a grown daughter, Miriam. He was a Jewish teacher whom Father unexpectedly brought home after a trip to Rotterdam. He had been on the point of turning himself in, after being shuffled from address to address for three months. At their first place, there hadn't been enough to eat; at the next place, they had to spend night and day in a shallow cellar; and at the last place, their hostess had lived in such obvious terror, that they decided they no longer wished to burden her.

Now they were living together in the camper and had finally found a little peace. The camouflage of branches and trees had been rearranged so that more light could enter the camper. Several fir trees had also been transplanted; now, one could pass within a few feet of the camper without seeing it. An efficient little petroleum stove had been installed to keep it warm in the winter months.

Mr. Liebstadt spent most of the day studying big books on economics, because after the war he planned to get a doctor's degree in this field. Mrs. Liebstadt did all the darning and sewing for the whole family. Miriam, who had been a secretary, did any jobs that needed doing, eagerly helping to can fruit and vegetables.

William—who now slept above the garage in Uncle Gerrit's one-room apartment—catered their food, and Uncle Gerrit dropped in occasionally to cheer them up with his jokes. John made a weekly trip to the city library or wrote to the University library to keep Mr. Liebstadt supplied with books.

In the evening, when the coast was clear, the Liebstadts joined the De Boers, visiting and listening to the news until it was time to return to the camper. As they walked back to the woods, the drone of bombers filled the night sky. In the beginning, Father worried constantly about Wallinga, for he would often come strolling across his land, jump the small canal between their properties, and then cut through the woods to find Uncle Gerrit.

But that problem had finally been licked. One day Wallinga complained that the turkeys were straying onto his property and scratching around in his crops. So Father overcame his distaste for the old Nazi long enough to go and see him and reach an agreement that a fence should be built along the ditch. Father and Uncle Gerrit were out there the next day putting up chicken wire, topped by a couple strands of barbed wire. Since then, whenever Wallinga wanted to talk to Uncle Gerrit, he had to use the road and come through the front gate. Now, at least, they could see him coming.

But this wasn't the end of the De Boer's involvement in hiding Jews. Rita wrote to tell them that the home where Marie's parents were hiding had become unsafe and that she was having no success at finding them another hiding place in the city. The De Boers couldn't very well leave Marie's parents in jeopardy—not after having fallen in love with their little girl. So Rita was told to bring them out to the country.

They arrived late one night when Marie was already asleep, and they didn't get to see their little daughter. Mother thought it was cruel, but the parents weren't even told that their child was there. They were given something to eat, had a cup of coffee, and were then taken to the Hoving farm. Mr. Hoving had built a small room in his attic with a little window that overlooked the fields. There, once a week they received a note from Marie, but without a return address. That way, if they were ever discovered, they wouldn't be able to reveal the whereabouts of their little girl.

Of course, Marie's sisters couldn't be left in Rotterdam after this. It was much safer out in the country, and they would also get more to eat. Next came Mrs. Liebstadt's brother. She pleaded with Father to help him because he, too, could no longer stay where he was. Father was unable to say no when a human life was in danger, especially if he were in a position to help.

Father couldn't very well say no to Mr. Peeks either when the farmer came to tell him he had two escaped Jews at home, but that it wasn't safe for him to hide them, as near as he was to the camp. Nor could he say no to Mr. Vander May when he called about three homeless puppies and asked whether Father could find a place for them. And he certainly couldn't say no to the mechanic who had gotten him two new tires for the car and who couldn't find anywhere to hide a Jewish boy in his pro-Nazi town.

Father always seemed able to find room somewhere. Otherwise, he could always turn to Mr. Hoving, who couldn't say no either. There weren't many people like the Hovings. Most farmers would have nothing to do with hiding Jews. They were either too scared or too concerned about their own comfort, and they found myriads of excuses for themselves.

Once in a while, however, unexpected help appeared. On the country road that ran behind the De Boer property lived two farmers, Fred Bouwman and Harm Barelds, who hadn't talked to each other for fifteen years because of a family feud. However, on the first day of the war they forgot their feud and became friends. It almost seemed as if they were trying to make up lost time, for they began doing everything together. When Father talked Harm Barelds into taking a diver, two days later Fred Bouwman came to the door asking Father why he hadn't come to him too. Didn't Father trust him? To show how well he trusted him, Father brought him two divers. Soon Harm showed up to let Father know he also had room for one more.

After supper one day, Garth Reinders came to the door. Of the people who had joined the N.S.M., Garth was one of the few Father still talked to occasionally, because he was an old school buddy. Despite his Nazi leanings, said Father, he wasn't a bad fellow, just misled. Father went to the door and gave him a rather cool welcome. Hesitantly, the man said, "I'd like to speak to you a minute, Everett, at least, if you haven't closed your door to me."

"All right," said Father. "Then step in for a minute. I hope you can understand why I haven't invited you over."

"But I've quit the N.S.M., if that's what you mean. I won't have anything to do with them anymore. I was taken in by their farm program. That's why I joined. But now things are getting worse fast! The Jews have never bothered me, and I see no reason to treat them like animals. Now they're going to start arming the N.S.M. too, and I won't have anything to do with that. I'm not going to face my neighbors with a gun in my hand!"

"Why are you telling me all this?" asked Father.

"Because I know that you've always been on the other side," said Garth Reinders. "You've got to help me, Everett. I've got a lot to make up for!"

Father grabbed his hand.

"Garth, you don't know how happy this makes me. I could never understand how you could identify with that pagan horde. But listen! The best way to make up for the past is to stay with the N.S.M. I'm your witness and when we're liberated, I'll testify in your favor. But the best way for you to help now is to go on being a good N.S.M. member. Keep their trust! And, in the meantime, keep your ears wide open and pass any unusual activity and information on to me."

Garth Reinders agreed, and suddenly he began to laugh ironically. "Did you hear the latest speech of Mussert, the leader of the N.S.M.?" he asked Father. "No, I don't suppose you listen to the villain. Well, he called on all Hollanders of good will—by which he means all Nazis, of course—to stop being spectators on the sidelines, and to lend a hand in the struggle. I'm not sure this is what he meant, but I'm ready to lend a hand."

After that, Garth Reinders went to every N.S.M. gathering and shouted along with all the other National Socialists. But soon he was hiding three Jews in his house, and they couldn't have found a safer spot.

All this activity could not, of course, be concealed from the older children. It wasn't necessary either, for by now they had shown that they could keep their mouths shut. Moreover, their help had become indispensable. Finding people to hide all the divers was only the first step. Ration cards had to be obtained for them as well as false I.D.'s. Some wanted books to read and others knitting and needlework. A few needed visiting and counseling, for their lives were tormented by fear and uncertainty, and most of them spent the entire day cooped up in small spaces. John, Tricia and Fritz were, therefore, kept busy running errands, and they could be counted on to do them properly. Besides, they didn't draw as much attention as Father would have if he had begun making regular rounds.

Tricia even struck out on her own. One afternoon she came home with Ada, a Jewish girl of fifteen, riding on the back of her bike. Tricia had found her wandering about on the outskirts of town. She had been told to flee from the place where she was hiding because the people had gotten word that a house search was in the offing. Unfamiliar with the town, the girl had no idea where to go. Uncle Gerrit had a suggestion: he knew of a widow who lived alone in a small house behind a stretch of state forest who was willing to help.

Later that evening John took Ada there, following the narrow dirt road that led to the well-hidden house. Not to be outdone, Fritz managed to get her an I.D. card. When he was sent out of class to do an errand at school, he stole Gracie Bouwman's card from her coat pocket. If Gracie had known what it was for, Fritz reasoned, she would have given it voluntarily. Besides, she was bold enough to go to the police and ask for a new one. Now if they asked her what had happened to her old one, she could truthfully say she didn't know.

He did get a reprimand from Father when he got home, but he interpreted the glint in Father's eye as approval. When Father had altered the I.D. card, he handed it back to Fritz and said, "There you go, for your little fugitive." That's how John, Tricia, and Fritz regarded Ada. She was their special responsibility.

A week later, Fritz arrived home from school to find Mr. and Mrs. Wiesel in the living room. It gave him a fright. Had his theft been discovered? But, no, they greeted him very warmly. When they left fifteen minutes later, they each had a Jewish child on the back of their bikes. The two children had been hiding in Uncle Gerrit's little apartment for the past two days without Fritz's knowledge.

"What did I tell you?" asked Father. "I knew Wiesel's heart was in the right place."

"You mean he's *helping* us now?" Fritz said, delighted. "Neat! I'll ... I'll ...."

"You'll nothing!" said Father. "You've seen nothing! And you'll go on behaving toward him as you always have. Understood?"

"I was just going to say that I'll never forget this," said Fritz, insulted. He could keep a secret as well as anyone, and if necessary he could lie like the Nazi Bureau of Information.

"At the height of all this activity, the De Boer house was suddenly selected to quarter a German officer. One Saturday evening, a German army car stopped in front of the house and out stepped a high-ranking German officer. At the front door he handed Margy a note and waited. Meanwhile, the chauffeur drove up the driveway to the garage.

The note that Margy brought to Father informed them that the local commandant had put their home at Colonel Schwalbe's disposal for two days while he and his chauffeur rested up.

There was nothing else to do, so Father went to the door to let the man in. The colonel saluted politely, introduced himself and made a gesture as if to shake hands, but Father pretended he didn't see it. Then the man said he was sorry to cause them trouble and that he would be happy with any room that they would be willing to spare him.

Father decided that the German better have the living room, so Mother opened the davenport and made it into a bed for the officer. The living room was the only room available, for Miriam Liebstadt had been moved from the camper to the guest room with a bad case of bronchitis. The chauffeur was given William's bed over the garage, and William moved in with John, sleeping on the floor.

They were all unsettled by the fact that now the enemy was right in the house with them, and it was a tense evening in the family room. The Liebstadts had to stay in the camper; the family couldn't listen to the radio broadcasts from England; and they couldn't play the piano because it was in the living room with the German. So they sat together quietly, reading a little and listening to every sound that came from the living room. But all they heard was an occasional cough. The man seemed to have a slight cold.

"Well," said William, "it won't bother him long once he gets sent to the Russian front!" There were rumors of a great setback for the Germans around Stalingrad. Hitler had ordered the city to be taken last October, but the Russians had held out all winter. Thousands of German soldiers had died in the frigid Russian climate.

Mother said that it wasn't right to talk like that about the man; they didn't even know him. She wanted to bring him a cup of tea, but Father told her not to bother. After a while she did it anyway. It didn't hurt to stay on his good side, said Mother. The man was reading a book, Mother told them when she returned. He had stood up when she entered and bowed when he thanked her.

"I think he would have liked to talk a little," she said.

He got a chance to talk the following morning. Trudy was the first one to come downstairs and opened the living room door a crack to peek in on the German officer. When she saw the man smiling at her, she stepped into the room and said, "Good morning, Mr. German. Look, my mommy made me a new dress."

Tricia heard her and hurried to snatch her away, but the officer said it was all right, he would like her to stay. When Trudy returned fifteen minutes later, she was beaming and had a handful of candies. She told them that Mr. German also had children at home—a boy and two girls. No one understood how they had talked, because the man spoke only German.

A short time later Colonel Schwalbe left with his car and chauffeur. Finally, Uncle Gerrit could relax. He had been overextending himself to hobnob with the chauffeur and keep him entertained so that the man wouldn't get bored and go for a walk. If he had, he might have stumbled across the camper. Now, too, they could get Marie downstairs. She had refused to budge when she had heard that there was a German soldier in the house.

That afternoon, however, the officer returned unexpectedly and surprised the children playing with dolls in a corner of the hall. Marie didn't see him coming, and suddenly she was confronted by the grey German uniform. Her terror was obvious. Maybe it was this that gave her away, or maybe it was her hair, which badly needed another bleaching. The German rested his hand on her head for a moment and looked into her fear-filled eyes. After he had divided a handful of candies among Hanneke and Trudy and Marie, he asked to speak to Father.

"Please keep the little Jewish girl in the house while I'm here," he said softly. "My chauffeur can't be trusted."

So the colonel wasn't just a heartless cog in Hitler's war machine. That evening Father had a long talk with him. He didn't tell the others everything they had talked about, but he did tell them that Colonel Schwalbe was not a National Socialist and that he was participating in the war against his will.

"Germany can't win this war," he had said. "It will be over by Christmas. We can't survive another Russian winter."

To hear this from a German officer was tremendously encouraging. What he said about the attitude of the Dutch was also encouraging to hear.

"I've been in France, Denmark, and Czechoslovakia, but the Dutch have shown the most resistance to National Socialist propaganda. Most Dutchmen seem determined to ignore us completely."

"But if you're against Hitler," Father had dared to ask him, "why are you in this war?"

"Wait and see. Wait and see," Schwalbe had said mysteriously. "You're fighting for freedom over here, and some of us officers of the Wehrmacht are fighting for freedom too. More I can't say. But one day you will think of me and of what I have said."

"Please don't repeat this," he had warned. "And be very careful around my chauffeur!"

The chauffeur, a big fat Prussian, spent the evening with Uncle Gerrit, who was trying to teach him some

Dutch. William sat by, watching. Heinrich wanted to learn Dutch because he had a girl in Haarlem, and he wanted to surprise her with a few sentences of Dutch.

"Can't be much, that girl of yours," Uncle Gerrit mumbled in Dutch.

Uncle Gerrit had almost put his foot in his mouth, for although the German couldn't speak much Dutch, he could already understand quite a bit. No, really, said Heinrich, she was a very pretty girl.

"Okay, Heinrich, repeat after me: 'A man is only as good as his word.' "

And Heinrich repeated after Uncle Gerrit.

"Not bad! At least, you're starting to sound better. I wish you would all get that into your heads!"

"Ja! Jawohl!" said Heinrich.

"Good. Let's go on. 'There's a time for staying and a time for parting, a time for weeping and a time for laughing.' Can you say that?"

William was writhing in agony, as he fought a losing battle to keep from bursting into laughter.

"Fine, Heinrich! Fine," said Uncle Gerrit encouragingly. "Here's another one that fits right in: 'He who laughs last, laughs best.' That's right: 'He who . . . .' "

Colonel Schwalbe had to leave early the next day. Father walked him to the car and shook his hand. On the other side of the car, Uncle Gerrit was saying goodbye to his student.

"Okay, finish this one," said Uncle Gerrit. " 'No matter how swift the lie . . . .' "

And Heinrich added triumphantly: " 'the truth is swifter.' "

"You're a good student Heinrich," said Uncle Gerrit. "Soon it will become even clearer!"

"Ja! Jawohl!" said Heinrich, smiling.

As he backed out of the driveway, the chauffeur leaned out of the window and quoted, " 'There's a time for staying and a time for parting.' "

Then he turned onto the road. The colonel waved once more, and the others waved back. Wallinga, who was just passing by, nodded good morning. "Old Gerrit had been right," he thought. "The De Boers weren't such bad people after all. They were really coming around."

CHAPTER TEN

A week after the officer's visit, Tricia was picked up by the Germans. After school she walked downtown with a couple of girlfriends, because she had dropped off her bike at the repair shop to have a tire fixed. It was impossible to get new tubes, and some people were putting pieces of rubber hose inside the tires, but that made hard going.

A three-day period of mourning had just been proclaimed by Hitler for the German soldiers who had fallen around Stalingrad. During the first months of the year, the German army laying siege to Stalingrad had been surrounded by the Russians. About 146,000 German soldiers had been killed and another 45,000 taken prisoner. Therefore, the Fuehrer had ordered everyone to observe three days of mourning: all theaters and cafes were to be closed, all flags were to be at half-mast, and all music, dancing, and loud laughter were forbidden.

The three girls, however, were not thinking of Stalingrad and the mourning Fuehrer at all. They had just finished a hard school day, which had ended with a tough algebra quiz, and they were carrying on like young fillies romping in a meadow. They were in a silly mood and were entertaining each other by trying to invent all kinds of puns, malapropisms, and garbled words.

"Who needs algebra? Algae have always done all right without any bras." "Algebra will turn us all into algaebrains." They giggled until they were weak with laughter, becoming more and more giddy.

"So you need a new bire on your tike, Biss De Moer?" "I think your bike is all tired out." "Yes, it's always getting deflatulated."

They were still carrying on when they passed S.D. headquarters—the German security police. Suddenly they felt strong hands laid on their necks. Roughly, they were hustled up the steps by two scowling soldiers and into the headquarters of the feared S.D. They were prodded up to a desk before a big fleshy German, who began barking questions at them. Suddenly one of the girls asked, "Is this the Stepago?" and they all broke into hysterical giggles.

Even the German couldn't keep a straight face. He exchanged a few words with the two soldiers, and the girls were lined up in the hall with their faces against the wall and their briefcases over their heads. They had to hold this pose for fifteen minutes. Then the fat German sent them off with a loud scolding, of which they didn't understand a word. The girls held their hands or hankies over their faces and sobbed hysterically, but they did so only to keep from bursting into laughter again. Finally, they were dismissed. Tricia's bike was finished and she quickly pedaled home to share her hilarious adventure with the others.

But when she got home, she found Mother extremely agitated. Only Fritz and the younger children were home with her, and she was frantically trying to clean up Father's desk while Hansie was hanging onto her skirt crying. She found a resistance newspaper between some other papers and quickly jammed it into her apron pocket. Father wouldn't be home for a couple of hours. Everybody else was gone too—except for Uncle Gerrit. But if Tricia wanted to know more, she'd better ask Fritz.

"And please take Hansie along; I can't get anything done this way!" Mother said distractedly.

A strange girl had delivered a letter to the door that afternoon, Fritz told her. Margy had taken it, and because Mother was taking a nap and Father was working out in the garden, she had put it up on the bookcase without saying anything. There it had stayed until about four o'clock, when Father and Uncle Gerrit had come in for tea.

Upon opening the letter, Father had leapt up out of his chair. The Germans might arrive any minute to search the house! he had announced. Then he had rushed out to move the divers to a safe place. Fritz had been ordered to go and find John and William, who were out delivering *Free Holland*, and tell them not to come home but to meet Father at the Hoving farm. Mother had to check through the house to see that nothing suspicious was lying around.

"What did the letter say?" asked Tricia.

"Wait a minute," said Fritz rushing to the window. From the road came the mutter of an automobile engine. But it turned out to be a dump truck. It chugged by slowly, its gas converter belching smoke.

"Twuk, twuk!" shouted Hansie, jumping up and down in Tricia's arms.

"It was a warning from Ron Mulder," said Fritz. "You remember him? He and Art Van Dyk hid here a few days? He's been in hiding for quite a while now. The Germans were looking everywhere for him. They must have really wanted him bad! John sees him once in a while, so he knows all about it. Yesterday Ron was told to get out as quick as he could, because the place he was staying at wasn't safe anymore.

"He figured that he had enough time to type a note to Art, but he had just written: You can always contact me through E. De B. You remember, he lives a couple of miles outside . . ., when the Germans pulled up in front of the house. Ron was able to get away through the back yard, but the dumbbell left the letter in the typewriter, and the Germans found it. So now you know why Mother's so upset!"

Yes, now Tricia understood. Anxiously, she looked down the road. "E. De B., a couple of miles outside . . . ." A good thing that he hadn't finished this sentence. But it was only a matter of time before the German police figured out who the letter referred to. What else could De B. stand for than De Boer? And then all that the

Nazis would have to do was check the local registers to find their address. Of course, Father would be listed as E.J. De Boer. Maybe that would help.

Mother returned from the studio with her apron pocket full of papers, which she jammed into the stove. She seemed less nervous now.

"No, Hanneke," she was saying. "You stay in the family room for a while. Tricia, Fritz, I'm worried about Marie. She senses that something is going on, and she's perched on the sewing basket beside the dresser and refuses to move. She's terrified! If she's here when the S.D. comes, she'll give herself away by her obvious fear. Do you know anywhere that she could stay for a little while?"

"Sure," said Fritz. "Put some warm clothes on her and I'll take her to Vander Brook's on the back of my bike."

Fritz ran outside to get his bike from the garage. Uncle Gerrit was just filling up a hole behind the shed; he must have buried something. He, too, thought it was a good idea to take Marie somewhere else for the time being.

"Are you staying around the house?" Fritz asked him.

"Sure, don't worry. You just take care of *your* job," said Uncle Gerrit.

"What if the Germans come? Won't that be dangerous for you?"

"Not for me," said Uncle Gerrit with a little smile. "I'm seventy-two years old, and every day I live is just so much icing on the cake. No one can harm me."

Fritz knew that no one would protect Mother more fearlessly than Uncle Gerrit. He pedaled as fast as he could, constantly scanning the road for the S.D. truck. Little Marie hung on behind him. During the whole trip into town Marie was silent, except for once, when she asked, "Fritz, what will my new name be when I get to those people?"

"Your new name?" asked Fritz. "You're not getting a new name, silly. You're still Marie De Boer, my little cousin. Right?"

"Oh," she said, wrinkling her nose. "My hands are getting cold."

"Put them in my pockets," said Fritz. As they rode on, he squeezed one of her little hands in his—to warm it up. He'd take care of her, he told himself. He would see that no harm came to her. She would be safe with Mr. Vander Brook, for he hated the Germans and wasn't afraid to say so in class. He was Fritz's favorite teacher.

It was almost dark when Fritz rang the doorbell. Mrs. Vander Brook was just closing the blackout curtains. Mr. Vander Brook himself answered the door.

"Well, hi there, Fritz!" he said. "Come on in. Is that your sister? Oh, your little cousin, hey? Well, bring her in too. Why so glum? You haven't been drafted to work in Germany, have you?"

"No, sir. But I'd like to ask you a favor. Could I speak to you alone for a minute?" He could see a tall girl standing at a doorway down the hall, listening.

"Sure, come on in," said Fritz's teacher. And he led Fritz and Marie into his study. "Honey, I'm going to talk to these two kids alone for a minute; they've got some deep secrets to share with me." He closed the door behind them. "Well, out with it, Fritz. I'm all ears."

He looked at them with affectionate curiosity. But as Fritz began to explain, his smile faded, and his eyes clouded over.

"So, she *isn't* your cousin," he said slowly. "Yes, now I can see she's .... Listen, Fritz, I'd really love to help but . . . well, I'm not out in the country, like you. I've got a neighbor living right next door who belongs to the N.S.M. So, well, you can understand the danger of . . . ."

"Oh, they won't notice a thing," argued Fritz. "She'll stay indoors. We've got one of those Nazis living next . . . ."

"Yes, but I've got kids at home. They'll see her. And if they'd talk about it . . . . You know what would happen to us if the Germans found her here? My wife and I would both be sent to Westerbork. They announced it a couple of days ago: anybody who helps the Jews will be treated like a Jew! No, I can't risk it. Besides, we don't have any room. That's just the way things are, my boy. Nothing much we can do about it . . . . It can't be all that bad living in those camps."

He got up and went to the door.

"You'd better be careful," he warned Fritz. "I can't understand how your father can . . . ."

He wasn't finished talking, but Fritz brushed by him into the hall, leading Marie by the hand. He was too disappointed to say anything.

The teacher opened the front door for them. His good

humor had returned.

"Well, Fritz, oso!" he said holding up his fingers in a *V*. "See you in school tomorrow. Don't shed too many tears over Stalingrad."

But Fritz's tongue seemed swollen and stiff. He stepped into the night without saying a word. The door closed behind him. He took a deep breath. Looking back, he caught a glimpse of Vander Brook's face at the window. Fritz quickly turned away.

"Can he keep his mouth shut?" Fritz asked himself. Suddenly he was filled with a deep doubt; he doubted everything. Here he was, standing out on the street with Marie, and Mr. Vander Brook wanted nothing to do with her. It seemed impossible. All those things that the man had said in school—was that all just talk? When it came to denouncing the Germans, he had more guts than anyone, but now . . . ?

He put Marie on the seat of his bike, but he walked himself, pushing her along. She hadn't said a word the whole time. But suddenly she shivered.

"Where are we going now, Fritz?" she asked.

"Don't worry, we'll find another place," he answered, but he didn't know where. He had been so sure of Mr. Vander Brook that he hadn't thought about an alternative.

"Mr. Wiesel!" he thought. But Mr. Wiesel's house was already overcrowded. "He absolutely cannot take another person in that little house!" Father had said. "Otherwise, we'll run into trouble." How about Gracie Bouwman's place? She lived around here somewhere. But he didn't know her address. What if he went to the wrong door?

At the corner of Park Street, he stopped, unsure of which way to go. He leaned on his bike and put his arm around Marie. The streets were completely dark. With the blackout, the street lights were, of course, never lit; and the houses too showed no light whatsoever. Would it always be like this? A plane went roaring by low over the rooftops—a German, of course. There were very few people out on the streets anymore.

Two women walked by talking about burnt oatmeal. It made pretty good coffee, one was saying. Across the street a German soldier clopped by, his heavy boots echoing loudly on the sidewalk. Fritz could hear him, but he could barely make out his shape. What should he do now? Take Marie back home with him? But what if the Germans had already come? It would be like turning her over to them. Mr. Wiesel was the only one he could turn to, overcrowded or not.

An old man came ambling down the sidewalk; Fritz could hear the tapping of his cane. Every so often, the man cleared his throat—a familiar sound! It was Fritz's art teacher, Mr. Biemolt. Maybe he . . . . No, forget it. Biemolt was such a scaredy-cat! Not only did he never dare to say a word against the Germans in class, he didn't allow his students to say anything either.

As his teacher approached them, Fritz said quietly into the darkness, "Good evening, Mr. Biemolt."

"Who's that?" the old man asked, stopping. "Is that you, Fritz? What are you doing in town so late? Who is that you've got with you?"

Fritz tried to answer, but all that came out was a

strange-sounding sob. Fritz was horribly embarrassed, but he couldn't control himself anymore. The disappointment and uncertainty were too much for him. His voice refused to obey.

"Come along, walk me to my house," said Mr. Biemolt. "It's only a couple of blocks down this way. You tell me what's the matter."

He took Fritz by the arm as if to support him, and when they got to the teacher's house, he lifted Marie off the bike. He ushered them inside, where they were greeted by Mrs. Biemolt, a tall, broad-shouldered woman. Fritz eyed her in awe. Mr. Biemolt was so small and frail, and his wife looked so large and powerful. But she was very friendly. And Fritz could hardly believe his ears. He had just begun to explain things when Mrs. Biemolt interrupted him.

"How awful! You poor dear! How about it, Fritz, couldn't she stay here with us?" She looked at her husband questioningly and he nodded at her.

"Of course! No need to say anymore. Marie De Boer, your cousin, you said? Fine! You're a good lad, Fritz. She'll be all right here. We'll take good care of her."

Mr. Biemolt accompanied Fritz back into the hall to the front door. Before he opened the door, Fritz looked up at him once more to thank him. In the teacher's eyes was the fearful expression that Fritz had seen so often at school when one of the students had made an anti-German remark.

"Not a word to anyone, okay?" Mr. Biemolt whispered. "No one must know! I can trust you, right? Of course I can. Yes, yes! It will be all right. God protect you and your family."

As he pedaled home, Fritz's mind was in a whirl. What a strange evening! Who was the scaredy-cat and who was the lion? Thanks to Mr. Biemolt, he could go home knowing that Marie was safe. Then he thought of Mother at home with only Uncle Gerrit and the younger children, and a fear that bordered on panic seized him. He pedaled faster than he had ever pedaled in his life. But when he rushed inside, winded, he found everything quiet and peaceful.

Hanneke and Hansie were in bed, and on the kitchen table a sandwich and a glass of milk awaited him. Mother and Tricia were sitting by the table as usual, and Uncle Gerrit sat in Father's chair with his glasses perched on his nose. He was studying the telephone book.

"There's quite a row of De Boers in here: A. De Boer, C.T. De Boer, F. De Boer. If the *E* wasn't too clear, it could be taken for an *F*. And look here: an E. De Bruyn and an E. De Braal. Maybe we've been worrying for nothing. There are probably dozens of possibilities."

It was some comfort, but it didn't relieve the pressure of waiting. The tension didn't disappear even when the Germans had not showed up after two days. Father and John and William did come home every day for a while, but they always had someone on the lookout. On the third day, Father hit upon the idea of calling Mr. Vander May.

Vander May dropped in to hear the story, and two days later he was back with good news. They could relax, for the letter hadn't even gotten into the hands of the S.D. As usual, the German security police had taken a

Dutch policeman with them on the raid as a guide and interpreter. He had happened upon the letter first, and right under the nose of the S.D. had slipped it out of the typewriter and slid it into his pocket.

"I'd say you owe that man an awful lot," said Vander May, "for it didn't take him long to figure out who E. De B. stood for."

"Yes," said Father thankfully. "Who knows how often and how many of us have been saved by such quiet, unseen acts of courage."

So the Liebstadts were brought back to the camper, and the Biemolts reluctantly gave up little Marie. The next day, William was back in the garage wrapping food parcels, and John started going to school again. Father wrote a note to his principal saying that he had been ill for a few days.

However, it took Father several days to get back to his old self after this episode. He had been deeply shaken by the whole business and had lost a couple of pounds.

"The next time something like that happens," he told Mother, "I'm not leaving you and the kids at home. That first night . . . ." He shuddered. "I can't take another night like that! I didn't close my eyes all night, thinking about what might happen to you."

Sometimes he would sit staring out into space, his eyes filled with worry. To John he said, "These are very uncertain times, my boy. Until recently I had a pretty good idea where to look for danger, and I could take precautions. But things have changed. We've come into contact with so many people, and it only takes one to slip up—like Ron Mulder. I almost wish we could all go into hiding."

"But things turned out all right, didn't they?" John said, trying to comfort his father.

"Yes, *this* time." He sighed. "Thanks to . . . thanks to . . . ."

Then he looked up at John, laughed, and said, "Don't worry, John. I know who to thank! The One who can strike the enemy with blindness. Still, that doesn't always make it easy."

From then on he didn't seem to throw himself into his work as he had before. He treated it almost as a burden, which he shouldered only because he had committed himself to it.

CHAPTER ELEVEN

Not until much later did the De Boer children find out exactly what had happened at the Wiesels. They knew the family had been arrested, for Fritz had brought the terrifying news one day when he arrived home from school pale with shock. Within the hour Father had left in the car, not returning until the next day. Fritz followed him all around the house, plying him with questions, but Father wouldn't tell him much of anything.

He only put his arm around his son's shoulders and said, "He's in very serious trouble, Fritz, but we haven't given up hope for your courageous teacher. I can only tell you this—and this is just between the two of us—we'll do what we can for him."

When Fritz looked into Father's eyes, it wasn't hard for him to stop his pestering for he saw there a determination that would yield to nothing. It gave him the feeling that the Germans could never overcome his father.

At dusk, Father left again, this time on his bicycle, and for a full week thereafter he spent more time away from home than at home. Then late one night, after Tricia and Fritz had already gone to bed, William, John, and Mother heard bicycle tires crunching on the gravel of the driveway. A few minutes later Father entered the room, exhausted and haggard.

With a hard, grim look in his eyes, he said, "Thank God, that's finished!" and he sagged into his chair.

Mother poured him some coffee, and John got him his slippers. William started rolling him a cigarette, but Uncle Gerrit ducked out a moment and returned with a cigar, which he had been saving for the day that the Germans would be defeated. "Here you go boss. Something tells me you've earned it!"

"My, my!" exclaimed Father. "Am I ever being spoiled! What a blessing that we still have each other. Poor Wiesel."

Then came the whole story.

The Wiesels' house had been raided in the middle of the night by three S.S. men and a Dutchman—Schram, the Jewhunter, as he was called by the police. They had rung the doorbell, but the soldiers had kicked in the door before Mr. Wiesel and his wife could get all their Jewish divers into their hiding place under the floor. The Jews, all adults, had immediately been taken away, and Mr. Wiesel had been shoved into his bedroom and subjected to a brutal interrogation.

The S.S. wanted to know how these Jews had found

their way from Amsterdam into Mr. Wiesel's house. But in spite of everything that the Germans did, Mr. Wiesel had stuck to his story that they had come to him straight from Amsterdam. And his Jewish lodgers, they found out later, had backed up his story.

While the Germans were searching the house, Schram stood guard over the prisoners. Wiesel was tied to a chair, and Schram took the opportunity to abuse his defenseless victim. It cost him something, however, for in his anger Wiesel managed to break loose and attack his tormentor. His wife came to his aid, wielding the base of a table lamp. Yes, that gentle, soft-spoken woman—that's how far that devil pushed her! The Germans had to come running to save their spy, but they didn't show much concern for him; instead they berated him for carelessness.

"Yes," said Father, "a traitor is despised even by those who use him."

As a result of the fight, however, the house search was cut short—a blessing for the two small children still hiding in the house. The two children, the same Jewish children that Mr. Wiesel and his wife had picked up from the De Boers, were never found by the Germans. They had hidden themselves in their space inside a hollow wall when the soldiers broke down the door, and they stayed there until neighbors came and found them the following morning. By then, Mr. Wiesel and his wife had been thrown into prison along with their divers.

A few days later, Father had contacted Mr. Wiesel through a prison guard and had set a plan in motion to free him. The prison doctor had agreed to give him something that would make him very sick and produce all the symptoms of acute appendicitis. This had gone according to plan. In the hospital, a couple of powerful young underground fighters had been standing ready to carry Mr. Wiesel to freedom. But the Germans had taken no chances. They had released his wife, but as sick as he was, they had shipped Mr. Wiesel, not to the hospital, but to the concentration camp at Vught. For the second time in his life, Mr. Wiesel was imprisoned in a concentration camp.

"Poor man!" said Father. "I don't know whether we'll ever see him again. I hear those camps are a living hell!"

They were all numbed by the account and sat together silently in a sad circle.

"We'd better not tell Fritz the whole story," said Father. "We'd better not tell him about the torture at least."

"And all because of that filthy worm, that . . . that stinking Schram!" exploded William. "He's got a few things to answer for!"

"Maybe more than you think," Father said, nodding. "Vander May has checked him out. He has been freed from all regular police duties so that he can spend all his time sniffing out Jews for the Germans. He gets a bounty of thirty guilders on top of his regular salary for every head he brings in. Apparently, he has already earned well over six hundred guilders in bounties!"

"That's more than twenty lives!" John cried in horror.

"That's right," replied Father wearily. "You might

say he's a murderer twenty times over."

"But . . . but," sputtered William, "we can't just let him go on! We've got to *do* something!"

"What do you have in mind?" asked Father.

"Do you have to ask?" demanded William. "That piece of human garbage better not get in my way! As far as I'm concerned, he's no longer a human being. We'd be doing the world a favor if we rid it of that piece of filth. Don't you agree?"

"No, William, not altogether," said Father. "We may never act out of revenge. That's always wrong. We may only act to save other lives."

"In this case, what's the difference?"

"Whoever rids the world of this man, or we could say, whoever brings this man to justice will have to give an account of what he has done. First, to God and, then, to his own conscience, and maybe, after the war, to a judge. And then he must be blameless. Would you dare to take the responsibility for Schram's death on your conscience?"

"Yes! Without a doubt, yes!" said William. "But why talk? Nothing's going to happen anyway."

"Well, as a matter of fact, since we're talking about it," said Father, studying his hands, "tomorrow we're having a meeting about this very thing. We don't want to make any snap decisions when it comes to a human life, so we're forming a kind of jury. It will take responsibility for decisions such as we have been talking about. And, Uncle Gerrit, I would very much like to see a wise old head like yours on that jury."

Uncle Gerrit had been very quiet. The Wiesel affair

seemed to have hit him hard. Now he gave a wan smile.

"You can drop the 'wise' if you don't mind. But, all right, I'll be there."

"While you're at it, what about that creep, Wallinga?" asked William. "He's not much better than Schram. This afternoon he was sniffing around here again. 'Aren't you better yet?' he asked me. 'How long have you been hanging around here?' So I told him that my school in Rotterdam had been bombed and that I've been looking for another place to teach, but I think he only half believed me. Pretty soon I'll have to leave here just because of that evil-eyed old goat. He should be put out of circulation too!"

"William, William! Now I do think that's hatred speaking," said Father. "If you were listening to what I was saying a minute ago, you would see that this is a completely different case. Would you be willing to do it? Before God, I mean."

William stared straight ahead and didn't answer. He seemed to be at odds with himself. But the next day he was waiting as Father and Uncle Gerrit returned after having been gone for several hours. He met them at the door.

"Did you reach a decision?" he asked.

Father nodded gravely.

"What about that creep next door?"

Father looked at him, and all he said was, "William, William."

In the middle of all this, the De Boers opened their home to another flier. He had come down several weeks ago near a neighboring town. He had been forced to jump when his bomber had been shot down by a German fighter, and his leg had been broken in the jump. A farmer had hidden him in his haymow, but he had not dared to fetch a doctor for several days, and now the leg wouldn't heal. The flier's foot was badly swollen, and infection had set in around the fracture. David (that was his name) needed better care than the farmer could provide, so he was brought to the De Boer house. They arranged to put him in the small first floor bedroom next to the stairs.

The flier was delivered under a wagonload of vegetables. While John and William stood lookout, Father and Uncle Gerrit carried him into the house on a stretcher. David, they discovered, was a young Jewish-American pilot. He was quiet, but very polite and gracious. After treating his wounds and feeding him, Mother couldn't resist ruffling his mass of unruly hair. For a moment the tension around his mouth relaxed, and sighing wistfully, he said, "I thank you, Madam. You're just like my mother. I feel quite at home."

An hour later, when Mother was fussing over him once again and began to fluff up his pillow, a pistol suddenly clattered to the floor. He quickly snatched it up again, and with eyes full of fear and determination, he stubbornly refused to give it up.

"The Germans aren't going to get me alive," he said. "I know what will happen to me then!"

After that, whenever Mother came into the room to help him, he tucked the pistol under his good leg.

Father spent a couple of days remodeling the house a little. Under the stairs, which passed between the studio and David's bedroom, was a closet that opened into the studio. Now Father nailed the door of the closet shut, put wallpaper over it and further covered it with bookshelves. Then he cut out the bottom part of the stairs to a height of five steps and installed hinges at the top so that they were invisible from the outside, especially when covered by carpeting. In the floor of the closet, he cut a large hole. Now when the stairs were folded up, a large black aperture gaped at them.

Next, Father and Uncle Gerrit built a wooden slide slanting down into the crawl space underneath the house. "There!" said Father. "Now if the Germans come to search the house, all we have to do is lift up the stairs and slide you underneath the floor boards, mattress and all."

David laughed, but he didn't seem entirely satisfied. "But what if the Jerries stay in the house?" he asked. "Then I'm caught like a rat in a trap."

The chance of that happening was more than slight. Occasionally, the S.D. made themselves a home for several days in a house that they suspected of being a center of underground activity. Then they would arrest everyone who came to the door. But Uncle Gerrit had an answer to that. He lowered himself into the hole. In the next four days, they lugged hundreds of pails of dirt out of the hole and spread them on the garden. Uncle Gerrit dug an underground passage under the foundation of the house to a clump of young spruce trees about thirty feet away.

He surfaced behind the clump of trees on the fourth day, very dirty and blinking like a mole. The opening was covered with a wooden trap door and topped with sod. There was very little danger that the passage would cave in, for the roots of the spruce trees laced the ceiling of the tunnel, creating perfect reinforcement.

Uncle Gerrit wanted to tell David about the tunnel himself, he was so proud of his handiwork. Father went along to act as translator. But Uncle Gerrit got impatient with Father, who had to keep searching for words.

"I'll tell him myself," Uncle Gerrit interrupted.

"But you don't know any English," protested Father, laughing.

"Just tell me the word for rabbit."

Father knew that.

"Listen, David," said Uncle Gerrit, gesturing. "You and I, zoom! in hole. Jerries in house. You and I, hippity-hop, hippity-hop—out in bush. Zoom! Gone. You understand?" Turning to Father, Uncle Gerrit said, "See? He understands me better than he does you!"

Spring was a peaceful time for the De Boer household. There was little war news. In Northern Africa the Americans were slowly but surely advancing toward Tunisia. In Russia, where the German army had been forced to retreat at several points because of the Stalingrad disaster, Hitler was preparing his spring offensive. The German-controlled newspapers held high expectations for this campaign, but most people were very skeptical. As the calm-weather season approached over the North Sea, hopes began to grow again for the Allied invasion, and more and more German sym-

pathizers began canceling their membership in the
N.S.M. for fear of eventual retribution.

The work of caring for the divers, however, had to go
on as usual. In fact, it was increasing every day, as more
and more people were being sought by the S.D. Those
who lived out in the country and who did not participate
in underground work, however, hardly noticed that a
war was going on. Everything went as usual: the farmers
were busy in their fields, plowing and planting, and the
children went to school as always. But John's school
work was suffering, perhaps because he spent so much
time writing letters to Rita.

He had fallen in love with her, but he hadn't seen her
for more than two months. The last time had been in
February, when she had brought them a young Jewish
couple, who had eventually found housing with Mrs.
Van Steen, the widow living behind the state forest,
where Ada, Tricia's little friend, was also staying. At
that time Rita had promised John she would see him
again in the spring.

Now it was already April. The front yard was bright
with tulips, and the calves were romping out in the
pasture, but Rita still hadn't come. She was too busy
now, she told John in one of her letters, but it looked as
if the time was approaching when she would be forced
to take a vacation, and then she hoped that the De
Boer's would save a bed for her.

John read between the lines. It was dangerous to say
too much in a letter, but John suspected that if Rita was
thinking about taking a vacation, she must be in danger.
He wanted to pack a bag and go to Rotterdam to find

out in person what he couldn't find out by letter. But
Father vetoed that idea. Now, whenever Rita's letters
were overdue, all he could think of was the dangers that
threatened her in Rotterdam, and he found it impossible
to concentrate on his school work.

One beautiful, summery day in mid-April, William
and John took a bike ride out to Mrs. Van Steen, who
had sent Father a note complaining about the Nathans,
the young couple whom she was hiding. The husband
refused to abide by her rule that he could go out only in
the evening. He roamed about at all hours of the day,
through the fields and along the roads right up to the
city limits.

"Just tell him the truth," Father had said to the
young men. "If he doesn't stop endangering the safety
of others as well as his own, he will be moved to a place
where he'll have to stay in a hole under the floor twenty-
four hours a day."

It wasn't a very pleasant duty, but this didn't seem to
bother William. In his usual carefree way, he was able to
enjoy the beauty of the moment, and he cycled ahead of
John whistling and singing so happily that it almost
grated on John. The last two days the mailbox had
yielded nothing, so he was especially worried about
Rita. In his thoughts, he followed her as she worked in
the hospital and as she cycled through the streets of
ravaged Rotterdam. That way, he seemed to be doing
something to protect her. He surrounded her with his
thoughts and prayers and love. Did she know that he
was with her in spirit?

When they came to the state forest, they had to go

another mile down a quiet, unpopulated forest road. Mrs. Van Steen's house was off the road a way, out in the trees. They parked their bikes against an old well overshadowed by a huge plum tree in full blossom. As they walked toward the house, a shower of small pink petals rained down on them.

Mrs. Van Steen, a kindly, stooped old lady, was working in the garden beside the house planting potatoes. Ada, Tricia's little fugitive, was helping her. Mrs. Nathan was sitting in the sun by the front door reading a book. Mr. Nathan had gone out for a walk—they had caught him in the act.

They were invited into the quaint little house and led into the living room. Mrs. Van Steen made a pot of tea, and William gave her the ration cards and the money to cover the costs of her boarders. This money was paid by the L.O., a secret organization that raised money for divers.

John also had a briefcase full of library books with him. He emptied it on the table and packed up the old books. Mrs. Van Steen was talking about her cat, who caught a rabbit recently. John would have enjoyed this visit if they hadn't come to do a distasteful task.

In about half an hour, they saw Mr. Nathan coming across the field with a big bouquet of spring flowers. The sight of the visitors didn't unnerve him in the slightest, and the tough message relayed to him by William seemed to make little impression on him. "What on earth can happen to me here?" he snorted. "This place is as quiet as a graveyard!"

"What about the farmers in the fields?" asked

William.

"Ah! They're too busy to pay any attention to me," scoffed Nathan. "And I always take a roundabout route on the way back, so they have no idea where I live."

"Nevertheless," said William emphatically, "you'd better understand that this is the last. . . ."

"Someone's coming!" Ada cried, rushing into the room. "He's almost here. A man in a grey suit!"

"Oh, that's probably the man from the burial fund," said Mrs. Van Steen. "You'd better duck into the bedroom because he always walks right in when I answer the door."

The Nathans and Ada quickly fled to their hiding place. William was simply going to stay put, but suddenly John leaped up and grabbed him by the arm, pulling him into the bedroom too. John had glanced through one of the small windows and had caught a glimpse of the visitor. He felt his pulse pounding in his throat.

"It's Schram, the Jewhunter!" he whispered in William's ear.

"You sure?" asked William.

"Positive!"

He saw William looking at him with that look he had seen a couple of times before—a hard, threatening look. He knew what William was thinking: "This is our chance, and we can't let it slip."

Suddenly, he felt queasy and weak in the knees. The room began spinning and tilting so that he had to lean against the wall for support. But it passed as quickly as it had come. He thought of Jake Vande Berg, and at the same time the lines of his poem passed through his mind:

> for not our own cause did we choose,
> nor do we stand or fall in our own frailty.

He felt new strength flowing into him, banishing all doubt and hesitation. Since the death sentence had been passed on Schram, Ron Mulder and Art Van Dyk had tried to ambush the man at least twice without success. He had escaped them each time, perhaps because he suspected something. But apparently it hadn't frightened him enough to make him quit his bounty hunting. This was their chance to save dozens of lives. They couldn't let it pass.

John slowly pushed open the bedroom door and peered through the crack. He pulled William into the room, for Schram was just getting back on his bicycle. They could see him through the living room window. As he left, he studied the house carefully one more time.

Mrs. Van Steen came back inside.

"He was asking for eggs," she said. "But I need them myself. What a queer duck! He kept rubber-necking to look into the house. And he asked me whose bikes those were against the well. I told him they belong to a couple of forestry workers clearing brush in the state forest. And then he picked up Mrs. Nathan's book that she left lying outside and kept looking at it. He's sure got his nerve."

They didn't hear her. All their attention was fixed on Schram, who was just about to the end of the long drive.

If he turned to the right, he would be heading for town along the lonely forest lane—a good place to . . . .

Yes, he was turning right! They charged for the door, but John held his friend back for a moment. He had suddenly taken the lead.

"Wait a minute," he said. "He can still see us between the trees."

"We'll let him get past the fork in the road," whispered William, "and then we'll pass him and stop him."

"Right!"

"But we haven't any weapons, and maybe he does. Can you jump him? You know judo!"

"Now! Let's go!" said John, sprinting for the bikes.

John got to the bikes first and went racing down the driveway. By the time he got to the road, William had dropped far behind. But then William began to catch up, as John paced himself carefully, keeping his eye on Schram, who kept disappearing around the bends in the crooked road.

Only when Schram turned left onto the heavily wooded stretch before the main road, did John begin to put all his weight into pedaling. William was shouting something, but his words didn't sink in. Thirty guilders per Jew—man, woman or child! He had collected his betrayal money for the last time, the bloody headhunter! It had to be done! And now! Anywhere on this stretch would do. The road was completely deserted.

John took the corner so fast that he almost lost control. He caught himself just in time, but not before a branch had gouged his leg. But he didn't slow down! He

looked down the road and saw nothing. Had Schram hidden in the woods? A ripple of fear passed through John. But when he rounded the next bend, suddenly the man was only a few hundred yards ahead, so he slowed down a little.

The Judas! He was riding with one hand on the handlebars, and he seemed to be directing a band with the other. He looked happy! In fact, he was whistling a tune, completely unaware that death was right behind him.

What's this? Second thoughts? More than twenty human lives on his conscience, and that was a month ago. Did that include Mr. Wiesel and his people? Besides, five men had condemned him to death: the doctor, the pastor, Vander May, Father, and Uncle Gerrit—all good men who were risking their lives for the same people that this monster was murdering. And now he had his eye on Mrs. Van Steen's house and on Ada and the Nathans. Maybe that's why he's so happy—that's another ninety guilders!

His bike leaped ahead. He had forgotten the plan. He saw the rabbit face look up, startled, and then Schram began pumping furiously. But John was already on his heels. He heard himself shouting, and Schram swerved aside. Now he was beside him, riding an arm's length away. Carefully gauging the distance, he launched himself at the scrawny figure, tumbling them both onto the grassy shoulder of the road.

He scrambled up and again threw himself on the man, grappling for his arm. He seemed to have forgotten all his judo. Now he had one of Schram's arms and twisted it behind his back. Something hit his foot—a revolver! So Schram had managed to get his hand on it. He kicked it to William, who was dancing around them, not sure what to do.

"Grab it!" shouted John. "Grab it! It's right by your foot!"

Didn't William hear him? Now Schram was starting to scream.

Slowly William picked up the revolver, and slowly he raised it . . . .

It was done. The body lay on the edge of the road. John felt as though he were moving in a dream, but he knew precisely what he had to do. First check the road. No one. Hide the bikes in the bushes. Three of them? Where did the extra bike come from? Of course. They had already dragged the body into the trees. He followed the drag marks, erasing them with his foot and kicking the pine needles back over the marks.

There was William; he looked ghastly. He was carrying dead branches and tossing them into a small gully where the tracks ended. John began to help him, also gathering last year's leaves and tossing them onto the pile. Then they began to walk back to the bikes. John stopped, leaning against a birch tree to recover his equilibrium. The bark was paper white with small dark flecks and delicate red branches protruding.

"William, what . . . ." he said.

"Don't fall apart now, man!" William pleaded.

Fall apart? He knew exactly what he was supposed to do. Why should he fall apart? They took the bike to the canal, and when the coast was clear, they flipped it over the side. A shame really! It was a fine bike. Then followed the long ride home. He remembered that part.

He also remembered laughing at Hansie and Hanneke. The kids mustn't know. William went looking for Father, but John staggered up to his room. He knelt by the bed, but he couldn't pray.

"For not our own cause did we choose—thirty guilders for Schram's new shoes." No, that wasn't right. But the refrain kept pounding through his mind: "For not our own cause did we choose—thirty guilders for Schram's new shoes."

Later he remembered that Father had sat beside him on the bed holding his hand, and he had asked, "He was a murderer, wasn't he, Dad? For thirty guilders . . . ."

"Yes, he was a murderer!"

"And it's war."

"Yes, John, it's war."

"And we're soldiers?"

"Yes, we're soldiers, son."

"For not our own cause did we choose. We march with Him . . . How did it go? We march with Him who has no shoes."

"Yes, John, you're a fine soldier, but—God forgive me!—you're also my boy, my Johnny-boy!"

Johnny-boy. Father hadn't called him that for a long time. And then he was sobbing.

Did he remember right? Had Father wept too?

CHAPTER TWELVE

Now that Mother was giving his injured leg daily care, David was looking better every day. The infection was beginning to disappear, his face was starting to relax, and the color was returning to his cheeks. Although fear continued to lurk in his dark, mournful eyes, he was much more cheerful than when he first arrived. When he had been hiding in the barn, he hadn't been able to talk to anyone, so now he appreciated the chance to talk a little. Sometimes David and John talked together until late into the night.

After the bike ride with William, John stayed home from school for several days. He wasn't really sick, but he was mentally exhausted, as if he had written endless series of exams. He couldn't stand to hear any music; even the singing of a bird sometimes set him off sobbing again. But as he sat chatting with David and saw the constant care his Jewish companion took to see that his pistol was always at hand, John felt a callus starting to cover the raw spot. Soon he could think back to what had happened in the woods without shuddering. He had done what was necessary.

That same night, Mr. Vander May had gone back to the spot with William, and they had reburied the body. They had taken Schram's wallet back home with them, and going through it, they had found notes that he had made while observing five different homes which he had suspected of harboring divers. They also found two anonymous letters addressed to the S.D. which the latter had apparently forwarded to Schram for further investigation. The people mentioned in the letters and notes were immediately warned to be careful.

A widespread investigation had been launched upon the disappearance of the S.D. collaborator, but Vander May knew that the Nazis hadn't found a single clue. No one had the slightest idea where Schram had been on the day of his disappearance, for he had worked entirely on his own and had always been very secretive. Even his colleagues had no idea what he had been up to. So John could relax on that score.

Nevertheless, he felt the need to talk about the affair with someone, someone who was completely trustworthy but who hadn't been involved in it from the beginning. He decided to talk it over with Rita. He knew what she would say, but he wanted to hear it from her own mouth. If she assured him that he had done the only thing possible, then the last remnant of doubt would be put to rest.

He didn't have long to wait. She wrote him that she

was taking a week's vacation at the beginning of May and asked whether John's folks could put her up. Mother and Father said they would be glad to have her, so now John was impatiently counting the days on his calendar.

In the last week of April, David was finally given permission by the doctor to hobble around the house. On Friday, April 30, came the general strike, and David spent the whole day peeking through the front window from behind the curtain. He saw the milkman go driving by with an empty wagon, grinning from ear to ear. Factory workers from town came cycling by in loud groups hollering at the farmers in the fields to drop everything and join the strike. Soon the children, too, came home from school because the teachers had also stopped working.

The strike had started spontaneously without any leadership. It spread as if a wind had blown through the country, whispering, "If there's no hope, if you're all marked for slavery, why go on? Drop what you're doing. Don't do another stitch of work for the Germans! They're dragging all your boys off to labor camps in Germany."

The thing that had touched it off was the announcement that all soldiers were going to be sent back to Prisoner of War Camps. The people had endured the persecution of the Jews, the forced labor in Germany, the labor camps for young men, and the food shortages, but this was the last straw. They weren't going to take this.

The same act of despair occurred simultaneously in

numerous towns and cities across the country. The factory worker dropped his wrench. The farmer unhitched his horses, tired of seeing all his work swallowed by the Germans. Bookkeepers threw down their pens, and machinists shut down their machines. And they all poured out into the streets.

They yelled at each other, "That's all they get out of me. I don't care what they do to me!" When they began to gather in the streets and heard others saying the same thing with similar determination, a note of celebration crept into their act of desperation.

Once again they got the taste of freedom in their mouths. What a joy to shake off the tyrannical yoke that had been chafing them for so long! They shouted defiance and execrations at their rulers. Suddenly they were no longer afraid to speak their minds. They loudly denounced the bootlickers and collaborators who were helping the Germans.

But the latter were not around to hear. Most of them had gone into hiding or were keeping their mouths shut. When the strikers noticed the timidity of those whom they had feared for so long, they grew even bolder. If they were one in their refusal to work, one in their discontent, one in their defiance, what could the Germans do? And if this became known across the channel in England, then wouldn't the Allies be encouraged to launch the long-awaited invasion?

The cows bellowed in the pasture and in the barn. They had to be milked, but the farmers refused to bring the milk to the distribution office—most of it went to the Germans anyway. So they churned it into butter or fed it to the pigs. Even some N.S.M. members were swept along by the mood of angry defiance and refused to turn in their milk.

A passer-by kicked over the milk cans that Wallinga had placed along the road to be picked up, and a white puddle gushed over the road. Wallinga came running out to the road screaming and quickly righted the cans, salvaging what he could. Then he stood guard over them until the milk wagon came to pick them up. But the driver whipped the horses right on by.

"I'm not picking up anybody's milk!" he shouted. "Least of all yours. Drink it yourself! And I hope you drown in it, you stinking turncoat!"

So Wallinga hitched up his horses to deliver the milk himself, for his helper had also joined the strikers. The dairy plant, however, was on strike too, and the strikers turned Wallinga away from the plant. As he drove his wagon back through town, he was razzed and mocked everywhere he went. He hollered back at the crowd, and when a little boy tried to climb up on the back of the wagon, he struck out at the boy with his whip. Seeing this, a group of striking workers mobbed him, pulled him off the wagon and poured all his milk over him. Then they threatened to toss him into the canal if he didn't shout, "Long live the Queen!"

Wallinga did it, but as he rode home drenched with milk, he was rabid with fury, and screamed curses all the way. When he saw the De Boer family with their neighbor Hoeks and a couple of the Hoving boys standing by the house doing nothing, he drove up the driveway and began ranting and cursing so hysterically that Father lost his temper and chased him off the yard.

That evening they excitedly gathered around the radio. What would the English say about the strike? Would they support it? Maybe they would call for a total revolt? Such a move would be disastrous, however, unless the Allies could immediately come to their aid. Yet, that's precisely what many people hoped.

When the voice of Radio Orange came on the air that evening, the announcer said that reports had come out of Holland about a critical situation in the country. In the name of the government-in-exile, he advised all ex-soldiers not to turn themselves in, but to go into hiding. But above all, he asked the people to remain calm and to wait.

That told the people enough. The day of liberation was not yet at hand. They had really been fools to hope for it. But they had wanted it so urgently!

The De Boer family went to bed that night deeply disappointed. A supply train went chugging through the darkness, heading for Germany. The next day the mailman again delivered the mail. The workers at the large nationalized factories in the big cities had not joined the strike. Father called up friends in various cities and learned that almost everyone was going back to work.

Meanwhile, the Germans had declared martial law: all strikers and anyone who participated in unlawful assembly in the streets would be shot down on the spot. Everywhere, German police trucks were rounding up prisoners and bringing them to the city jails. A few kilometers away, three farmers were executed right before the eyes of their families.

But in the part of the country where the De Boers lived, people still were not going back to work. The noon train was attacked at the bridge by a pack of exuberant boys who pelted it with rocks. Only Mr. Hoving was out in his fields working, and he was plowing under the crop that the Germans had ordered him to plant. The crop could have brought him a good profit, but he hated it because it made him a slave of the Nazis.

Something had to be done, however, to restore sanity, Father insisted, or else the strike would result in tragedy here as it had elsewhere. So he sent the boys and Tricia out on their bikes to call together all the people who were part of the local underground. Most of them showed up very quickly, their eyes full of anticipation, for they hoped to hear good news. They knew that Everett De Boer had good sources of information.

The meeting became a very lively affair. The studio was crowded with people, and the debate became very heated. John could hear their raised voices outside. He was sitting at the side of the house pretending to read a book, while he kept an eye on the road. Sometimes the voices grew so loud that he could hear what was being said.

"It's folly! We've got to wait until the time is ripe, until we're really needed. What can we do now? We have no weapons, no leaders, no plans. It's no longer a united uprising. In other parts of the country the strike is over. I say go back to work before people are killed!" John recognized Father's voice. Father was sitting near the partly open window.

"Stop? Just when we get things rolling? I won't hear of it! I'm sick and tired of kowtowing to those bloody Krauts. If none of us go back to work, we'll stymie them. They can't very well line up the whole country against the wall. We've given in to them too easily—you used to say so yourself!" That was the booming voice of Hoving, fearless as ever.

Then everybody began talking, and John couldn't follow the debate anymore. After a while, the door suddenly flew open and everybody came stomping outside with flushed faces. Apparently they had not been able to come to an agreement. Hoving was the first to jump on his bike and, steamed up as he was, he almost ran down Garth Reinders who came racing up the driveway.

"Scatter, scatter!" he yelled. "The Germans! Everybody get out of here." He was gasping for breath. "The Germans are on their way. Wallinga—he was in town—he called them. I ran into him. He noticed all the bikes in the yard. He was mad because you chased him off the yard!"

As he gasped out his story, he kept his eyes fixed on the road.

"Beat it, as quick as you can! They'll be here any minute! Wallinga, that dirty . . . ." But they didn't hear the rest of his sentence, for he was already racing his bicycle back down the driveway.

Father began giving orders: "John, take Hanneke and Marie and get moving! Cut across the fields and through the woods to the back road. Fritz, you take Trudy and follow him. Tricia, you stay with Mother and look after

Hansie. No, there's no time for questions, do what I tell you! Clothes? Who cares about clothes at a time like this? William, run to the camper and get the Liebstadts out of there! You can find some place to hide. Start walking, Mother! I'll catch up. Uncle Gerrit! Uncle Gerrit!" Uncle Gerrit emerged from the shed with a revolver in each hand. He passed one to Father.

"You go with your wife," he said. "I'll take care of David."

"But Uncle Gerrit, I can't just . . . ."

"Hurry up, beat it!" shouted Uncle Gerrit. "You've got a job to do. Now go! And God go with you."

When Father ran off after the others, Uncle Gerrit hurried into the house and locked the door behind him. Then he closed and latched all the windows and also locked the kitchen door.

"David!" he shouted, and he opened the stairway trapdoor. Then he heard the squeal of brakes on the road, and he ran into the living room. There they were already: a large truck loaded with German soldiers was just turning up the driveway. They seemed to know exactly which house they were looking for. No wonder. That had to be Wallinga sitting in front with the driver. Sure enough, he was getting out!

Now he was looking past the house into the orchard. Had Everett been able to make it to the woods yet? If the Germans gave chase, they could still catch up easily. Unless they were held up!

There was only one thing to do. Uncle Gerrit reached into his pocket, and as the soldiers dismounted from the truck, he closed one eye, took aim, and pulled the trigger.

Bang! A hole appeared in the front window. Ha! That wasn't so hard. Again. Bang! Kind of funny, the way the soldiers scattered like a bunch of spooked turkeys. They scrambled for cover behind the truck and in the shrubbery. But there stood Wallinga, the Judas, staring stupidly at the house. Didn't expect that, did you, you knucklehead! See, we can fight back. You better head for cover, dear neighbor. But, wait a minute, didn't he deserve to die? More so than those soldiers?

Whang, whang!

What? It was David firing, stretched out on the floor by the window. Attaboy, David! His dark eyes flashed in his pale face.

Bang! That was mine. Whang! That was David again. He knew how to shoot, that boy, for Wallinga clutched his chest and toppled over like a felled tree.

Look out! They were shooting back. Oh, no, another shattered window! Boy, those bullets really whined. Those must have been bullets whizzing by a few seconds ago, too. What was that? Was the captain or the sergeant or whoever blowing a whistle? Oh, oh! They were moving, running around the side. Bang! Drat, missed! Now they'll try to get in on the other side of the house.

"David!" shouted Uncle Gerrit. "You here. I go there." He pointed toward the studio as he ran in a crouch toward the hall. Sure, go ahead, shoot away. That clock had seen its best days anyway. Sorry, Everett, your house is a mess. Everett must be long gone by now. Seventy-two is a ripe old age. I'm afraid you're not get-

ting much of a prize in me, boys. If you hit me, you'll only send me to heaven a little sooner.

Ha! I knew it. They're at the studio windows. Bang! A shame—that beautiful window. Sorry, Everett. Where was that guy? Did I hit him?

What was that terrific explosion in the front? Were they throwing hand grenades? That German wasn't coming back. Maybe he was lying dead under the window.

But it was getting high time for them to make their exit. He'd better get David. He hurried back into the living room, but David had disappeared. One more shot through that broken window wouldn't hurt. Bang! Wow! The Germans were giving it back one hundred fold.

"David!"

Where was he? What was that crackling in the family room? Was the house on fire? Over there, a head at that window!

Bang! Gone.

One more for good measure. But the gun only clicked. Of course, out of bullets! They had to get out right now.

Another tremendous bang—this time from the studio!

"David! David!"

No answer. Maybe in the kitchen.

There lay David, staring at the ceiling, his legs folded under him. When Uncle Gerrit tried to lift his head, his hand came away covered with warm blood. He was dead—that beautiful boy—dead!

Uncle Gerrit sobbed with grief and fury. He flung his pistol at the window as a German soldier dashed by. Then he crawled toward the trapdoor on his hands and knees. He could see that the studio was also burning now. He shut the trapdoor behind him and let himself slide down into the dark hole.

There he lay in the dirt, his mind completely blank, until he became conscious of pain. Sparks were raining down on his head and hands, and a large piece of wood came crashing down into the hole beside him lighting up the crawl space with its flames. He pulled himself into the mouth of the escape tunnel and lay still again. Then the smoke drove him further and further into the tunnel until finally he bumped his head against the trapdoor.

Only then did he recover and realize where he was. He lifted the hatch carefully and peeked outside through a crack. Flames were belching out of all the windows of Everett's beautiful new house—the dream house that he had designed himself.